FISH CAMP

Kate Banco

This is a work of fiction. Names, characters, places, and incidents either are the product of the author's imagination or used fictitiously. Any resemblance to actual persons, living or dead, events, or locales is entirely coincidental.

ISBN: 978-0-692-18636-7

DEDICATION

To my family and loved ones,

 Without you, my life would be ordinary and joyless. I am grateful every day for your presence in my life.

Thanks to my drinking buddies at Starbucks for your encouragement and honesty. You help me start each day with a smile.

Most of all I dedicate this work to my granddaughter Clara, you are our future. Your generation is our hope for a better tomorrow to bring down the walls we've built.

ACKNOWLEDGMENTS

The author acknowledges the many immigrants who risk their lives every day to provide a better life for their families. You enrich our lives by sharing your culture, language and culture. This novel wouldn't be possible without the many stories immigrant students share with teachers in the classroom. May your journey bring what you are looking for, and may your challenges be few.

We change, whether we like it or not
-Ralph Waldo Emerson

FISH CAMP

Chapter 1

The hot sun beats down on the metal roof of Tía Elena's house. It's mid-summer in Baja, Mexico and the dry heat is too much on normal days, let alone when a cloud of grief hangs over this house. On days like today I don't know if the heat makes the grief worse or vice versa. Anger and disbelief cause the bile to rise in my throat. My thirst is intensified by the heat, but I don't want to leave my room to get a glass of water. I stare at the ceiling with disbelief. Memories of that last day with my family roll down my cheeks. Now, what should I do? Tía Elena can't support herself and now she depends on me.

My family left San Felipe Friday afternoon but never made it home to the ranchito three hours south. My mother, father, brother and sister, killed in a careless accident, they told us. He knew that curve so well, he traveled that road so many times before.

When I said good bye to my family I didn't realize it would be the last time I would ever speak with them. My dad wanted me to return to the ranchito and help out. Maybe his real reason was he didn't want me, his naive seventeen-year old daughter, staying in town. I'm sure my dad worried about me hanging out with boys from the beach. I imagine my father remembers how he felt when he first met my mother at the age of seventeen. My mom told me many stories about how desperate they were to be alone when they first met. They were always trying to sneak out from under the watchful eyes of family.

The federales arrived early Saturday morning and told us they didn't suffer, it was over in an instant. A rancher found my father's SUV in a ravine. That means they were there all night, and no one noticed. It's sickening to think of them lifeless in a ravine full of cactus and snakes. I wonder if a snake found their bodies before that rancher.

They are all gone. My mother, father, brother and sister gone in an instant, a careless accident the police say. My father is such a careful driver I can't believe he caused an accident. When I asked permission to stay behind it saved my life, I wanted to stay on the beach with my friends. Now I'm an orphan because I wanted to have fun.

I can see Tía Elena is devastated and heartsick. Her favorite brother and his family are dead and she is now alone and responsible for me. All of this is beyond either of our comprehension, it's obvious one of us needs to be the strong one, and I don't think she is capable. It may have to be me. She has been sobbing non-stop since we received the news.

Tía Elena calls to me softly and asks me to please come to the kitchen. I don't want to leave my room because I know if I do, I can't pretend my family is sitting in the kitchen eating breakfast. I can't pretend nothing happened to change my life forever. Tía Elena calls me again. I drag myself off the bed, I want to give up and fall to the floor and sob, throw a tantrum and kick my feet. I don't want to act like a grown up. It's too soon.

Tía Elena has a death-warmed-over look, as if she died and no one told her, as if she is walking around like one of the calaveras during the Day of the Dead. I could put a fancy hat on her and she could be La Calavera Catrina, the iconic image of a wealthy woman, dressed as a skeleton with a fancy hat. The image shows social class doesn't stop death, we all die whether rich or poor. I have to look away to erase those images from my mind. She is the only one left of my immediate family and I love her dearly, I don't even want to imagine her death.

"Sarita, come here please and hold my hand. I am so weak I'm not sure I can continue. You know I am not a strong person and my health is poor. I need to ask you to do something," Tía Elena whispers.

Her sobbing is uncontrollable to the point I think she may vomit. Her eyes look like they cannot possibly cry any more tears. Her hands tremble in mine.

"Sarita, please forgive me for what I am about to ask," she says.

"Tía, I'll do whatever you need me to do. Tell me what you need. Do you want me to do your work at the bakery? I can go do that. I know you can't go to work for a while. I can do your job for you, I'm sure they would let me do that," I say.

"No, I don't need you to work for me, I need you to do something else," she cries.

"Tía, what is it? Anything, just tell me," I say.

"I need you to go to live with your uncle in the States. I need you to go work in the States to make enough money to help me," she says as she puts her head on my shoulder and sobs.

My first thought is I didn't hear her right, she can't be asking me to leave. Why would I leave her? She needs me, I need her. It's impossible to think I would leave Baja and go north to live with an uncle I don't know. Impossible!

Tía Elena's body shakes with sobs, it's out of control. She is falling into such a state of despair I fear she will need to go to the clinic. I decide I will do whatever she asks me to do.

"Tía, stop crying. If you need me to leave I'll leave. I don't want to, but if it's what you need me to do, I'll go north."

The sobs stop and she lifts her head to look me in the eyes, "There's no other way. I don't think I can work to support the two of us and there are no jobs for you here in San Felipe. You have to go."

Okay, I'll do it, but if there is any chance to stay I want to stay, I mumble to myself.

We hold each other for a long time, neither of us wants to let go, "You are my family, Sarita. I shouldn't ask you to do this, but I don't see another solution. Please forgive me."

I nod my head and wipe my tears with the back of my hand. It's decided, I'll go north to live and work with an uncle I've never met. I realize she has all ready invited Juan to come to the house.

"Sarita, you need to listen when your cousin, your primo Juan, comes to explain where you'll cross over," Tía Elena says with a worried look on her face. It seems like the dark circles under her eyes turn a deeper shade of a purplish color as reality sets in.

Why do I need to listen to primo Juan? I need time, no one is giving me time. Everyone wants me to do something for them. I know it's hard for Tía Elena, but it's hard for me too. I need someone to hug me like my mom always did. I need to hear my Papá's voice. Papá, Mamá I miss you. I can't do this. I don't know what to do.

As the days go by I'm more worried about Tía Elena. The news is a shock to us both, but I've decided I'm the one who needs to make a sacrifice.

I think Tía Elena has regrets, I know she misses her brother so much. I know she wishes she could have invited them all to stay, if she had, they would still be alive. If only she had known what was about to happen. The last conversation with my Papá is driving her crazy I can tell. She is probably thinking she could have prevented the accident, that it is her fault. I know she told her brother to wait, and not take the road back late at night. I remember her telling Papá it is less dangerous during the day. I have the same regrets, I wish I had been with my family. I wouldn't feel so much pain right now and I would be with them.

Before they left I heard my dad say to Tía Elena, "Hermanita, you know how many times I've driven this road at night. Too many times to count. I know that road like the back of my hand, I know every curve and every pothole. Don't worry about us, you worry about mi hija. Take care of her for me."

Tía Elena told my dad, "You know if I were able to support myself I'd ask her to come live with me, get her out a bit, let her get to know more people. But you already help me pay rent and buy groceries, I couldn't take care of her the way someone should take care of a seventeen year old girl," Tía Elena said with a sigh.

"Hermanita, you never have to worry about money. We will always take care of you. Don't you worry about anything," he said as he gave her a big hug and a kiss on the cheek.

As a child Tía Elena was unable to attend school due to recurring bouts with fevers and headaches. Her parents had gone to many doctors including a curandera or healer. The doctors said there was no solution. By the age of ten she had a partial paralysis in her right arm. She struggled and tried to go to school to continue her studies. But Tía Elena decided she would much rather stay home and help her mom with the daily chores. Her cooking skills improved while her academic skills slipped further and further behind. As she grew older her father found her a job a few hours a week helping in a local bakery. It would never be enough to support herself, but with help she was able to live on her own.

Papá swore to her he would care for her since the day of their dad's funeral. Tía Elena had been able to live with her dad following her mother's death a year earlier. Between the two of them they got by with her dad's pension and her small salary. Now what would she do? She couldn't support herself let alone a seventeen-year old. The only solution would be to send me to live in the US with her other brother Enrique. There are no jobs in San Felipe where I can earn enough to support us. After all, I would have to help take care of Tia Elena and support myself.

"Sara, it's the deal you've got. It's not anything your parents wanted for you. They didn't plan on leaving you orphaned.

A few hours later I hear Tía Elena speaking with someone in the kitchen. I want to know who it is but don't want to leave my room.

"Sarita, come on to the kitchen, your cousin Juan is here. You need to listen to Juan and he will help you cross over the border to the US. Your cousin Juan is here to help us," Tía Elena says.

I don't want to leave my room, but I go to the kitchen. I look at my cousin sitting across the table. It's obvious by his blue t-shirt and saggy blue pants he wants everyone to know his affiliation with his gang. All the gangs dress in monotone colors, blue must be the Norteño's color, so I guess he is a Norteño.

Gangs don't really interest me, it isn't an issue on the ranchito. The gangs are more popular in the border towns and Juan is just another gang member to me, wearing the colors and walking the walk of a gang member. It's hard to tell if he is a wannabe or actually involved in a gang. Bigger and more violent gangs appeared in recent years. They terrify the people, demand pay offs and kill people in border towns. I know of Norteños, Sureños and other larger gangs. The newer more powerful gangs even terrify the military and the police. Some of the bigger gangs are controlled by drug cartels.

Anger makes my head ache as I listen to Juan. I fiddle with the glass of water Tía Elena places on the table in front of me. I know I need to help, but it's still not fair. Losing your whole family in one day isn't fair. Moving isn't fair and most of all moving to a place where I don't speak the language well is the worst. How can I make a living when I don't even speak a lot of English? How would I send money to Tía Elena? High school was easy for me and I earned high grades in my English class, but speaking the language is a lot more difficult than taking tests in school. Once a week I met with an American tutor online. English has been my passion since I was little. Now I'm going to the US but this isn't how I wanted it to happen.

"Okay, tell me more of what I need to do. I'm listening. Who is helping me cross the border?" I ask.

"Samuel and Esmeralda are taking you. So, after they pick you up you need to start acting like part of their family. They speak Spanish so you won't have any problems. They have permission to cross the border for shopping and they take their kids to medical appointments often," Juan says.

"How does that work, if they don't have papers, how do they cross over? What if things go wrong? What is the worst that could happen? Will they arrest me?" I ask with a look of bewilderment on my face.

Juan ignores my questions, "If they suspect something, they will detain you. If they find out you aren't their daughter, they will send you back across the border. If that happens you will need to call this number. Keep it with you. Samuel and Esmeralda have never had that happen to them. They help cross people over because they have the right paperwork. You have to practice being their daughter and everything will be okay."

Easy for you to say. How can I pretend to be someone's daughter? I've just lost my family and now you want me to pretend to be happy and to be a part of another family, I thought.

"Why do Samuel and Esmeralda do this? Do they want to help people?" I ask.

"Yes, of course," Juan smirks.

"What do you mean? Why are you grinning like that?"

"They do it for the money, Sara. It's a business."

My jaw drops and my face turns red. "How much does this cost?"

Juan mumbles the answer.

"What? I can't hear you. Speak up," I say with authority I don't feel.

"Twelve thousand five hundred dollars."

"What? Who pays that?" I ask.

"Sara, you do. You'll live with Tío Enrique in Oregon. He will give you a place to live and eat. He will find you some work and you start paying off the debt, poco a poco you will pay it off," Juan explains.

"What happens if I don't pay it?" I ask.

"You don't want to do that Sara. You don't want to know what happens," Juan says.

"They might as well kill me, I want to die anyway. I'm not afraid of dying," I say as I turn away from Juan.

"They wouldn't kill you, they need you to work off the debt. They would kill or torture someone else, like Tia Elena. You can't do that to her. She needs you, you know that."

"No, they wouldn't do that! They couldn't do that. How would they know if I pay it or not? Who do I pay anyway?" I cry thinking about the nightmare in front of me.

"The coyote who arranged this is the person you pay. Samuel and Esmeralda get paid by him, so you don't have to worry that they'll turn you in either because they want to get paid," Juan explains.

I realize everything he tells me is bad news. As he looks out the window, I can see he is preparing his words carefully. I already demonstrated he needs to convince me to go. But all he has done is tell me I would be an indentured servant. How long would it take me to work myself back to freedom?

Juan continues to tell me more details, "They, like many other Mexican citizens, work for one of the maquiladoras or big American companies located near the border. It's like a no-man's land in between the US and Mexico. The landscape is filled with huge manufacturing companies. Samuel and Esmeralda have worked for a maquiladoras for many years, and the company gives them temporary passes. They use the passes to cross over for medical problems or shopping. Samuel and Esmeralda have a young child who needs therapy for his legs, so they go once a week to appointments and once a week to shop. He needs special medications and they need to get them across the border. They cross over all the time. You will take the place as Rosario, their teenage daughter, the next time they cross over," Juan says.

"Do I need to start wearing my hair like Rosario?" I whisper.

"No, but she does wear glasses, here take these and put them on," Juan says as he hands me a pair of reading glasses.

"How can I wear someone else's glasses? Won't everything be blurry? I don't want to!" I hear myself screeching.

Juan looks at me and glances back at Tía Elena. He then slams his fist on the table and bellows, shocking me into silence.

"Do you want to hear your other choices? Do you want to hear about the young girls who don't make it across the border and end up trafficked for sex or used as drug mules? You are one of the lucky ones, you get to ride across with a family. No walking in the desert for you, no hiding in landscaping equipment for you, never knowing when they will let you out. I know of two young boys who were stuffed into lawnmower bags and put on a truck. It took them two days to cross the border. The driver didn't know they were on the back of his truck and he left it in the parking lot at Home Depot. They were so dehydrated when they found them, they needed to be hospitalized. When they recovered they were deported back to Mexico. Did they give up? No, because their Mom was waiting for them in Texas. They had to try again. They walked across the desert all night with a coyote. It took them three days to get across. Only half the people who try to walk across the desert make it. Is that what you want, to die in the desert? When they did make it to Texas their Mom had moved to Oregon and they had to find their own way to Oregon from Texas. I don't think I need to tell you details about what can happen to two young boys traveling that far alone."

"Sarita, por favor. This is the easiest way. I don't want you walking across the desert," Tía Elena pleads.

"So I don't have a choice," I grab the blue plastic glasses from Juan.

"Perfect! You look different already, Rosario."

"What? Why are you calling me that?" I take the glasses off and put them back on again. A refection in the mirror in the kitchen shows me I don't look too bad with glasses. I feel like I'm going crazy.

"You need to get used to it, that's your name from now on. Or at least until after you cross into the US. Start listening, if you hear someone call you that name. Your birthday is different also, you are now a year younger and your birthdate is September 7. So start practicing. If I ask you when your birthday is you better know the date."

"Okay, my name is Rosario and my birthday is September 7."

"Make sure you have the right year. Where were you born?"

"Rancho Gu.... I mean Mexicali. Mexicali, is that right? Where was Rosario born? I don't remember. This is so difficult trying to act like another person. I don't want to go, it's not fair," I cry and run back to my room.

I taste the salty tears on my lips. My shirtsleeve is the closest thing to a handkerchief and works well to wipe my face. I wonder how things can get any worse.

Chapter 2

I sleep very little that night. I need to be responsible for myself and Tía Elena by going North to live with an uncle my dad never liked. I'm finding it hard to be happy or care about anything, let alone sleep.

My room in Tia Elena's casita is off the kitchen, it's small and hot. I smell coffee brewing and the aroma of fresh tortillas. Of course, Tía Elena is trying to make it easier for me by filling me with food, but I don't want to leave my room. If I stay right here no one can make me leave. I can eat very little and ask for nothing from Tía Elena. If I can find work in San Felipe we can get by. I just know we can.

I grasp the gold chain around my neck, the one my dad had given me on my 15th birthday, it's all I have left. He told me it was 14 karat gold. The locket holds a picture of my family, this is the most valuable thing I own. It's something I'll never give up. How bad will things have to be for me to give up the only thing I have left from my dad.

"Sarita, come it's time to eat. You need to eat enough to be strong for your trip," Tia Elena says after knocking on the door.

"I'm not going, Tia. I'm not going. I've decided I'll stay here with you and I'll find work. We'll get by. I don't think I need to go live with Tío Enrique. Whose idea was this anyway?" I say stamping my foot.

The door opens and Tía Elena walks in without turning on the light, "Sarita, you need to go. There is no work for you here. I can't pay my rent with what I make in the bakery and I won't have any extra for you. Your father always paid my rent and bought my groceries. I'm so sorry, but you can't stay here," Tía Elena says with tears in her eyes.

"No, Tía. No, I don't want to go, there must be a way. I can give classes, or sell things at the market. I'll do whatever I need to do. Please don't ask me to go!" I plead.

"Sarita, you need to go. I can't keep you here. Your trip is already organized. Your cousin Juan already has the details. You don't want to make him angry, he can get very mean. Believe me, I've seen him and his friends get very angry. I hear a car outside, let's get you some breakfast and we don't want to make them wait. They are so kind to help you," Tía Elena whispers.

"Kind, Tía? They aren't kind, it's a business. They make money doing this. I feel like you are sending me away and I haven't done anything wrong. Can't you see that?" I ask.

"I have coffee and warm tortillas for you. Come and eat, I don't want to argue any more. It is our last day together. I don't want to be angry with you," Tía Elena turns and leaves the room.

I can't believe I need to be the strong one. Why won't anyone listen to me? A horn honks and I grab my backpack. I have no other ideas, I have to leave San Felipe. Tears roll down my cheeks for the second time today. I don't bother to wipe the tears away. As I walk through the kitchen door I see Juan seated at the table drinking coffee and eating fresh tortillas and eggs.

"Juan, please, there must be another way. Can't I try to stay here and work? You do it, how do you make a living? I could do what you do," I whimper.

"Sara, we have already discussed this. You have to go, there's no choice, and believe me, you don't want to do what I do," Juan wipes his face with the back of his hand.

"What do you do? Why is it so bad?" I ask.

"Let's go, they are waiting outside. You need to get across the border before noon. It gets very busy around noon. If they go across right after the morning rush many of the guards are on break and they don't stop as many cars. Come on, let's go now!" Juan raises his voice.

"Sarita, por favor. Don't make your primo angry. You need to go. I don't want you to go either, but the plan is in place. We need to follow through," Tía Elena says with tears in her eyes.

"This never would have happened if I hadn't stayed here for an extra week. I should be dead along with the rest of my family."

"Don't say that Sarita please. I can't bear to think that. You are all I have left of my brother's family!"

"Now, I am my own family, I have to work and leave my home. If I have to leave I don't want to see you cry, Tía. Please don't cry. I'll go so I can help you. But that is the only reason."

"Sarita, I'm going to say goodbye now and leave the room. Remember, I will always love you, and be thankful for your help. Nothing can replace our family, but sometimes we have to do things we don't want to do. I would go with you if I could, but I'm not strong like you. I've been sick and I can't travel far. Please take care of yourself," Tía Elena leans in to give me a kiss on both cheeks and walks away sobbing.

"Okay, now that that's over, let's get going," Juan says.

"Give me a minute, I don't want to meet my new parents with tears. I need a minute," I say as I walk to the bathroom to freshen up.

"Okay, but hurry up. They'll start charging more if you don't get out there in the next five minutes. I'll wait for you outside," Juan says.

I close the bathroom door behind me and look in the mirror. My eyes are red and swollen, I am almost a different person. I don't resemble anything of what I looked like a week ago. I turn on the cold water faucet and splash water on my face. As I turn to grab a towel I see the hand-crocheted towels on the rack. I remember when my mother gave those to Tía Elena one Christmas. I dry my hands and fold the towels. I start to walk out the door but hesitate. I turn around and grab the two handmade towels and stuff them in my backpack. Tía Elena won't mind, she'll understand. I push open the front door and walk outside to my new life, and to never look back.

"It's about time, Sara. We've been waiting for twenty minutes," Samuel says.

Juan waves me over to the station wagon and signals for me to get in the back seat. I open the door and look in. Two younger children are asleep while a toddler sits in a car seat drinking from a bottle.

"Get in, Sara. Come on. We're wasting time," Juan pushes me into the car.

"Wait, you aren't coming with us?" I ask.

"No, you know that. We already discussed what you need to do. Do you have that phone number I gave you? Call me if you have any problems when you get across the border. Samuel will give you a bus ticket to Oregon. Remember it's not close, so you will need to get some food and water before you get on the bus. Here's $50 to help you get to Oregon. Use it to buy food and to call me if you need help," Juan hands me the money and gives me another nudge to get in the car.

"Samuel vámonos. Let's go," Esmeralda says as Samuel puts the car in gear. "We need to get going so we can cross over at our normal time. We're already late. There's a blanket on the seat if you want to sleep."

"Adios, Juan. We'll be in contact," Samuel waves as the car pulls away.

From my backseat I see familiar sites out the window, I see the stores and houses flash by as we leave town. We turn and cross over the Avenida de Mar Cortez away from the Malecón. The bakery where Tía Elena works is already open, aromas of pan dulce spill out the door. I wish I could stop and leave her a note to let her know how much I love her, but it's too late, I am already moving into my new life as Rosario. We stop at the Pemex station on the corner before leaving town.

I want to cry out and say, "I was here with my father so many times. I wish I could see him one more time," Tears run down my face and I hide under the striped blanket.

"Rosario, stop crying. You don't want the crossing to be difficult. If they see you're crying they may question us. It is almost two hundred kilometers to Mexicali. You have two hours to get over your grief and pretend you're our daughter. Can you do that?" Esmeralda says as she hands me a tissue.

I reach for the tissue and reply, "Yes, I can. It's been very difficult. I don't want to do this. If I could stay here I would."

"Well, it's already in motion now. Learn to live with what life has given you. We don't all get what we want," Esmeralda says.

I wipe my eyes and blow my nose. It's obvious no one is going to take care of me or make sure I'm okay anymore. They don't care how I feel or if I'm sad. These are just a couple of business people putting in a day's work.

The station wagon pulls out of the Pemex station and we head north down the Calzada Chetumal. I lean back in the seat and try to relax as I watch the dry, arid land pass by. What will Oregon be like? Will it look like this or will there be mountains? As I start to relax and think about my destination I drift off to sleep.

I haven't slept a full night since the accident and my body relaxes as the car speeds along Mexico State Highway 5. It may be a blessing to rest before we cross the border. I won't have an opportunity to rest once I am on my own in the States.

Chapter 3

I sleep most of the two hundred kilometers and wake up when one of the youngsters in the car punches me in the side. I jolt awake and find the eyes of a five year old in my face.

"Move over, you're taking up too much space. You can't sleep on top of me," yells the little one.

Disoriented, I sit up straight. I had slumped over and ended up resting my head on the small child. I rub my eyes and look around.

We're driving through a city and Esmeralda turns around and says, "Good, you're awake. We're almost to the border, you need to start paying attention to what we tell you."

"How far is it?" I ask.

It has been my goal for a long time to take a trip to the United States for a vacation or to study English. I love learning English, but this isn't how I imagined my trip. New York City is where I would like to go on vacation, not to the Caléxico bus station. My plans to go to New York to see the sights and go to the Statue of Liberty do not compare to my trip to Oregon to live with my uncle and travel by bus to get there.

"A few more minutes, see that line of cars up ahead? That's where we start to line up for the crossing. You can either sit back and pretend you are sleeping or sit up and answer whatever questions they ask. What do you want to do?" Esmeralda asks.

"I'll pretend to be asleep, if they ask me questions I'll respond. Can you make sure your son doesn't hit me again? Will he say anything if they ask?" I say.

"No, we tell him to never say anything when we are crossing over. He knows better than to speak up. Right, Beto?" She says as she turns to look at the five year old sitting next to me.

"Sí, Mamá," answers the boy.

"Don't worry about him. You remember your name, place of birth and birth date. We carry the papers. If they ask to see your papers, turn to me and ask for them. They usually don't ask once they see our permission to cross from work," Samuel says.

I slouch down in the seat and try to calm down. With eyes half closed I peek out to see how far away the crossing is. I try to sing a song in my head to calm my fears. My mother taught me that trick. As a student I had anxiety about taking tests. My mother taught me to hum or sing so no one could hear. I start humming the song Colors. My best friend Maria and I had loved to sing the song during the 2018 Fifa football championship. I smile when I remember Maria singing and dancing on her bed. Then my memory is interrupted when I get punched in the side.

"Move, idiota," The five year old Beto punches me again and brings me back to reality.

"Stop it. Don't punch me. You have enough room. You move over," I say.

I look over to see Beto trying to push me over in the seat.

Samuel turns around and smiles, "That's right Beto, you know what to do."

"What? You think it's okay that he punches me? I asked you to tell him to stop," I raise my voice.

"He knows what to do, follow his lead," Esmeralda reassures me.

We move closer to the guard booth. Three cars are in front of us. I peek out of the blanket to see what to expect. What I see is scary. A tall guard with sunglasses has a machine gun over his shoulder. His finger is on the trigger as he leans into the cars to question the passengers. He spends a few minutes looking at documents. He then hands them to his co-worker while he talks with the driver. The other guard scowls as he looks over the documents and types names into the computer in the guard booth. Above them is a camera. It reacts to movement in the car, they are recording everyone. What a scary idea. They'll never let me across.

They direct the car in front to pull over to a lane and wait for further instruction. I hope that won't happen to us. Samuel puts the car in gear and moves up until the guard signals him to stop. He reaches over to get the papers from Esmeralda.

"Buenos días Señores," the guard says without smiling. "Documentos por favor."

Why do the American guards speak Spanish I wonder, I thought the minute we cross the border everything would be in English.

Samuel hands him the papers and answers, "Buenos días."

"How many people are traveling today?" The guard asks switching back to English.

"Mi mujer, los cuatro hijos y yo."

"Muy bien, un momento," He answers as he hands the paperwork to the other guard.

"Excuse me sir, your daughter doesn't usually travel with you does she? We show you usually travel with the little ones but not your older daughter. Special occasion today?" the guard says as he stares at me.

At that moment, the five year old punches me in the side and yells, "Move, I told you to move over Rosario. Move away from me."

"Beto, stop it right now. Leave me alone," I yell back at the child.

I watch the guard, but out of the corner of my eye I could see Beto pinching the toddler through the car seat. The child starts screaming at the top of her lungs. Samuel and Esmeralda turn around to chastise both Beto and me. Esmeralda reaches to comfort the baby.

"Stop it right now. Rosario, you asked to come along today. We don't have these problems when we leave you in school. We should have left you in school today. Move over and give Beto room."

I answer, "Fine leave me here, you always spend more time with Beto. He always gets to go shopping. I always have to stay home. Let me out and I'll take the bus home."

"No, you aren't going anyplace. Sit back and be quiet. Help your mother with the baby. It's easier for you to reach her. Let Beto sit next to the window, you move over and get the baby to stop crying or we will hold up this line for too long," Samuel says.

"Sir, please pull over to the lane on the right. The guards there will check out your car for contraband."

Samuel grits his teeth and pulls the car into the indicated lane, "Don't say anything," whispers Esmeralda.

"Good morning everyone. Could you all please step out of the car? We need to take an extra look," The guard says.

I want to grab my backpack and run back to San Felipe. I don't know anyone here and I don't trust Samuel and Esmeralda. If the guards question them and find out the truth they'll have problems. If they find out I'm trying to sneak across the border as their daughter I'll be sent back across to Mexicali. I can hardly breathe, I reach in my backpack for the phone number Juan gave me. Will I need to use it? Will I be left in Mexicali on my own?

Terror runs through me and I almost blurt out, "They kidnapped me, I don't want to go to the States. I belong back in San Felipe with my family."

"Señorita, come this way please," The guard motions to me. Why were they separating me from the others? Will I be arrested? Were they going to arrest Samuel and Esmeralda too? What about their kids?

The guard approaches me and starts asking questions, "Why are your parents going to Caléxico today? Did they pack any extra boxes or bags in the car?"

"We are going to a doctor appointment for my brother, he has problems with his legs. They go almost every week. I don't see any extra bags, why do you ask?"

I look over to see guards asking Samuel and Esmeralda questions while another guard searches under their vehicle. I start to feel sick, sweat beads up on my forehead. I look away from the car and through a big glass window, inside I see a guard walking with two people in handcuffs. They look terrified and I don't want that to happen to me. I think up something to tell the guard and wonder how many people get handcuffed every day. How many people get caught while crossing the border and end up back here in handcuffs?

"Are you nervous? Why are you sweating? You look very nervous," The guard tells me.

"No, I'm not nervous about this. I'm nervous because my Dad might find pictures of my boyfriend on my phone. He doesn't like my boyfriend," I lie.

The guards finish the search. The guard questioning says, "I hope your dad doesn't look at your phone, or should I tell him? I'm a dad too."

I shake my head and say, "No, please don't. He can get very angry."

The guard smiles, turns and walks away. From where I am questioned I look over to see everyone sitting in the car waiting for me. Esmeralda motions to me to hurry up. I wonder if it would be better to stay in Mexico and not cross the border. What would happen if I turn and run into the crowd and disappear? Would they try to find me? I just want this to all be over and wake up in my own bed back at the ranchito. I walk to the car and get in.

"It's about time Rosario. Let's get going before they decide to ask you more questions. What did you tell him?" Esmeralda whispers.

"I told him I was nervous you would look at my phone because I have pictures of my boyfriend. I told him you don't like my boyfriend."

"What? You don't even have a phone. What if he had asked to see your phone? That was a stupid mistake. We told you to stick to the story. Tonta! You almost ruined everything," Samuel snarls.

"He didn't ask to see my phone. It worked out. Stop yelling at me."

I feel proud of myself. I lied and got away with it and now I don't owe Samuel and Esmeralda anything after they drop me off. Samuel pulls the car out of the parking spot and moves forward past the guards while giving them a smile and a wave.

"You almost ruined everything. Don't say another word," Esmeralda says.

Everyone sits in silence, even Beto. When they exit the bridge ramp and enter the highway I let out a huge sigh of relief. I look back across the bridge to see the giant Mexican flag waving me good bye.

"Did you plan that? Did you have Beto punch me so it would distract the guard? Do you know that Beto pinched the baby? Did you tell him to do that?" I say in disbelief.

There was no answer from the front seat. A few miles down the road Esmeralda turns and says to me.

"It worked didn't it? You are in the US aren't you? Listen, this is our job and we know what to do. If it had been a different guard we would have done something different. Your little lie about pictures on your phone could have ruined everything. That guard will remember us if he sees us again. We won't be able to cross over at this time of day for a while. Sometimes we start yelling at each other and cause such a disturbance that they don't want to do anything but let us by. You'd learn too if you had to do it for work."

I can't believe they used their five year old. He learns from his parents it's okay to fool border guards. It seems like they are setting him up to be a coyote or smuggler when he's older. In the last few days I had to grow up fast and now I have to learn how to survive on my own. These people don't want to help me, they just want the money and they are willing to make their own children lie.

"Now what happens? We're across the border. What do I do? Where do you drop me off?"

"We drop you at the bus station in town. That's where our help ends. We have a ticket for you to get to Los Angeles. From Los Angeles you have another ticket to get to Woodburn in Oregon. We transport and drop, nothing more. You need to find your way after that," Esmeralda answers without a smile.

This moment had been coming since we left San Felipe, but I'm not prepared to be on my own yet. I hope they will help me get some food or give me more instructions.

"Where do I buy a sandwich and a drink. Juan told me to make sure to buy food before I get on the bus," I ask with the hope they will take time to help me.

"At the bus station they sell food. We'll drop you there and you are on you own after that," Samuel says.

I realize the time has come for me to be on my own and I'm not ready. I don't like Samuel, Esmeralda and their mischievous children but the alternative is worse. I will be all alone. I want to cry. I want to jump up and down and throw a tantrum and refuse to get out of the car. But, I know I can't do that, I have to make that first step. I'm in the States on my own. This is something I didn't plan to do, but here I am. C'mon, you've got this I tell myself. Get out of the car.

"What if they don't understand my English? What if I don't know what to do? Can you help me?" I ask.

"No, we need to get back to Mexicali to collect our money. We have things to do," Esmeralda says.

"Okay," I start to give them thanks and Samuel pulls up and stops.

Before I can look around to gather my things he has the door open and waits, "Out you go. Let's go, no time to talk or cry. Let's move it," Samuel says in a loud voice.

I watch as the old station wagon pulls out of the bus station leaving me in a cloud of dust. This is it, I'm on my own now. The main door to the bus station is in front of me and I make my way to the door. As I enter the bus station a strong smell of disinfectant overwhelms me. I notice a cleaning woman mopping the floor and moving toward the rest room, she obviously is Mexican or of Mexican descent. I follow her in to the ladies room and look around. The fresh smell of Fabluloso is in the air. It is a mixture of a pine scent and perfumed scent. The woman must have mixed the two cleaning liquids. The smell almost gags me, but I go in to the stall and lock the door. I hang my backpack on the hook and sit down. I'm alone. I don't know anyone here or anywhere except San Felipe. My uncle will pick me up in Woodburn, but I don't know him. All I know is that my father never liked Tío Enrique, and I doubt I will either.

CHAPTER 4

The bus station is dirty and people don't look up when I pass by. I could disappear and no one would notice or care. No one knows where I am or who I am. Who will help me if I need it? Alone, again that feeling creeps in to my mind. I want to sit down and cry. I hope through some magic when I open my eyes this is all a bad dream. It's not a dream. I am in a bus station in Caléxico and if I want to survive I need to buy some food. I look for a clock, I need to find out the time and what time my bus for Los Angeles leaves. I hope no one asks me a question I can't answer. If I don't make eye contact with anyone I think people will leave me alone.

I walk up to the snack bar and look at the menu. Hamburgers, sandwiches, chips and sodas. Nothing looks appetizing to me. I grab a cold sandwich, an apple and a pineapple juice. Ten dollars for one meal, that seems so expensive. Juan gave me fifty dollars and I need to make it last until I get to Oregon. Today is Tuesday. My bus won't arrive in Woodburn until Thursday night. How can I make my money last until then? I'll put the chips and juice back. I pick up a bottle of water and look at the sandwich. If I only get the sandwich and water it will be $8. If I only eat one meal a day it will be $24 and I'll have $26 left for emergencies. I need to make it to Oregon on one sandwich a day. I can refill my water bottle at the drinking fountain. My plan will work if I don't get hungry or have any problems along the way. I never ever dreamt I would be in a position where I have to budget money for food.

I open my backpack and put the sandwich and water inside. The crocheted towels jump out at me reminding me of this morning with Tía Elena. I hope she is doing okay, I know she's worried about me. I lift one of the towels and wrap my sandwich, I squeeze the water bottle into a corner of my pack. It's lunchtime. Now, I wish I'd have eaten the breakfast Tía Elena made me. I'll have to wait until I'm on the bus. I can take a little hunger.

I look around to see where my bus is. The destination of each bus and departure time appears on the board on the wall. Los Angeles isn't on the list of destinations. I look down at my ticket.

The ticket says Caléxico...San Diego...Los Angeles. Do I need to take a bus to San Diego first? Juan didn't explain that to me. What if I get on the wrong bus and don't have enough money to get to Oregon? What should I do?

A short man in workman's clothes approaches me. "Need help?" He asks.

"What, I'm sorry I don't understand. Can you repeat that?" I say.

"Do you need help?" He said pointing to me as he spoke.

"Yes, I am going to Los Angeles. I have a ticket but I don't know which bus I need to take," I explain in my best English.

"Can I look at your ticket?" He motions me to hand him my ticket. He grabs the ticket and starts to run away.

My feet are stuck to the floor like glue. I can't move. I open my mouth, but no words come out. In that moment I hear a whistle and someone yelling.

"Robert, get back here with her ticket! You know we'll catch up with you on the bus. Give her the ticket," Another man in a uniform yells.

I turn to see a police officer yelling at the man with my ticket. Robert drops the ticket and runs to the exit. The policeman walks over and picks up my ticket.

"Here miss, I think this is yours. We know Robert, he tries to do that to every young person who travels alone through this bus station. He never gets very far," The police officer smiles. "You need to be careful if you travel alone. Where are you headed?"

"Headed?" I'm puzzled.

"Where are you going?" He asks.

"Oh I'm going to Los Angeles, but I don't see the bus. Which one is it?" I ask in the best English I know gripping the ticket in my hand.

"San Diego, you need to go to San Diego first, then change to another bus to Los Angeles. Come, I can show you. Look up there on the board, the bus to San Diego leaves in ten minutes from door number four. Do you see where it is on the board?" He points to the board on the wall.

"Yes, now I see it. Thank you. Thank you for helping me. I didn't know I needed to go to San Diego first," I answer with relief.

"What is your final destination?" he asks.

"Final destination?" I'm puzzled again.

"What is the end of your trip?" He asks.

"I'm going to live with my uncle in Woodburn, Oregon. I think it will take two days by bus."

"Oregon, wow. It will take you at least two days. Do you have your tickets for the whole trip?" he asks.

"Yes, I have a ticket to Los Angeles and then another ticket from Los Angeles to Oregon. My friend gave me my tickets, but he didn't tell me I need to go to San Diego first," I explain.

"You should buy some food to take with you. It will be a long trip. You are about my daughter's age. I don't think she could do this on her own. You are very brave," he says with a smile.

I don't understand everything he says but I answer "Yes, I have a sandwich and a drink for the trip," I return his smile.

"Let's get you on that bus before it leaves. Come on I'll walk you to the bus," he says as he walks toward the exit door.

"Thank you, but you said door number four, right?" I hesitate. I watch as he continues to walk to a different exit.

"Just follow me, this is a shortcut, you won't have to wait in line. Don't talk to strangers in bus stations. Always look for an employee or police officer, understand?"

"Yes, I understand. I'll be careful."

I follow the police officer to the door marked taxis. Why are we going to the exit for taxis? I stop and hesitate, should I follow him? He waves to me from outside the door. I take a few steps toward the door when another man grabs my arm and starts to pull me toward the police officer.

"Help me! He's trying to take me! I don't know him, please help!"

I look to the police officer for help but I see he has his handcuffs in his hands and is reaching for my other arm. They both have me in their grip and I start screaming.

"Help me, help me. This isn't a police officer. My name is Sara, please help me."

Just as I scream my name they both drop my hands and run. They run down the street and disappear. I sink to the ground and start to sob. I don't care if I embarrass myself, I was almost kidnapped. I don't want to be here alone. I want to go back to San Felipe. A woman approaches me and starts to help me up. I look at her pregnant belly and wonder how she can even bend over.

"Here, come over here and sit down. You've had a fright. Did they really try to kidnap you?" She asks.

I sob and try to get the words out, "Yes, I think so. They both grabbed my arms and were going to handcuff me. I think if I didn't scream they would have kidnapped me. I don't want to be alone any more."

"My name is Patty. Where are you going?"

"Speak slowly please, I don't speak a lot of English. I'm going to Los Angeles, but I need to go to San Diego first I think."

"Yes, that's right, I am on the same bus with you. Let's sit together. I'll make sure no one comes near you until we are in Los Angeles. Let's get some food and get on the bus."

I walk with Patty back to the snack bar where she buys four sandwiches, chips, cookies and two cups of coffee. She offers me a coffee.

"Sara, are you ready to get on the bus? Let's go find a seat?"

I stop and say, "Wait, how do you know my name?"

She hesitates and says, "Silly, you yelled out your name when you started screaming. I thought that was a great idea. It scared them away when you screamed out your name."

We walk to the door marked for San Diego. We climb aboard and show the driver our tickets. He motions to us to find a seat and closes the door. I look at the other passengers on the bus and feel relief to hear many speaking Spanish. A bit of relief sweeps through me now that I'm on the bus. I walk down the aisle looking for an empty seat. All the seats are full except for two near the back of the bus. I take the seat next to the window and Patty sits down next to me.

The bus pulls out and I lean back on the head rest. I want to stop and think but things happen so quickly. This morning I was in San Felipe and now I'm on a bus going to San Diego with a complete stranger. This is so weird.

"Sara, where are you going?" Patty asks.

"To Oregon, to live with my uncle," I reply.

"Wow, that's a long trip. Are you traveling alone for the whole trip?" Patty continues to ask questions. I look out the window and try not to cry. I need to get used to the questions but it is still too soon. I try to form the words in English that I will have to repeat for the rest of my life.

"Yes, I'm alone. My family was killed in a car accident a few days ago."

"Oh no, I'm so sorry. I can't imagine what you are going through, and then those two jerks tried to kidnap you. You've had a bad day!"

"Jerks? What are jerks?" I ask.

"Idiots, or as you say in Spanish, idiotas?"

I smile and say, "I think it's been a bad week."

Patty laughs and says, "Okay, a bad week then."

"Where are you going?" I ask.

Los Angeles, I'm going to surprise my boyfriend. He doesn't know I'm coming. Won't it be a surprise?" She says as she points to her pregnant belly.

"It would be nice if someone was waiting for me there in Los Angeles but I'm going to Oregon," I say.

"I'm not sure he'll be waiting for me. Here, you can sleep if you want, I'll watch your stuff. You don't have to worry, I won't fall asleep with this baby kicking me. She has been kicking me all morning."

"When is your baby due?" I ask.

"This week, I hope I make it to LA before she's born." Patty laughs.

"You're brave. What if your baby comes on the trip?"

"I'm sure she won't be the first baby born on a Greyhound bus," Patty laughs again and wiggles in the seat trying to get comfortable.

"Are you hungry? I have plenty to share." Patty opens the bag to offer me food.

"I'm not hungry, but would like a juice. Do you have one to share?" I ask.

"Of course. Let's both have something to drink. Before we get to San Diego we can share a sandwich. What do you think?" Patty asks.

"That's a great idea," I mumble.

Chapter 5

I wake up with a jolt. The bus slows down and pulls into the San Diego bus station. Other passengers stand and gather their things.

"Dónde estamos? I mean, where are we?" I say as I wipe my eyes.

"In San Diego, we have 15 minutes before we leave for Los Angeles. Our bus is over there. See where it says LA North?" Patty points.

"Okay, do we get off and get on the other bus now?"

"Yes, but we have time to use the rest room first. Or one of us could go save a seat and while the other one uses the bathroom. I hate the bathrooms on the bus," Patty explains.

"Okay, do you want to go first? I'll go get a seat on the bus. Hurry up please."

Patty stands up and says, "Yes, I want to go first. This pregnancy makes things more urgent." Patty walks down the aisle and turns to look at me.

"Sara, if I don't make the bus don't wait for me. I plan on getting on that bus but sometimes things take longer than I expect," Patty says as she pats her belly,

"Oh, I want to travel with you, I'm safer with you. Hurry, I'll use the bus bathroom," I say.

"Okay, I'll try. See if you can get us a seat in the front of the bus this time."

I follow Patty down the aisle and jump off the step of the bus. I look around and think that I might like to visit San Diego someday. Today, I don't have that luxury of time, nor do I know if I'll ever be able to visit San Diego. The coffee aroma in the air makes me want to buy a cup of hot steamy liquid. In the sunshine it's warm, but a cold shiver runs down my back. The cold grips me like an ice shower. I tremble and look at the bus in the next lane. I take out my ticket and walk toward the bus where people are already lined up. I step aboard and walk past the full seats and find two empty seats together. As I pass two young Mexican men they call out to me in Spanish.

"Mamacita, ven aquí. Siéntate conmigo," and then they laugh. I walk past them and don't respond. I sit in the aisle seat leaving the window seat open for Patty. I hope Patty hurries up, I'll feel safer with her next to me. An older woman asks to sit in the window seat next to me but I tell her it's saved for my friend.

I look out the window to see Patty talking to a man with dark sunglasses. He is showing her a map and pointing to the bus. He must be asking where the bus is going. Patty turns and gets in line to board the bus. What a relief, I feel better now. I don't want to travel alone.

Patty squeezes herself between the seats until she sits down next to me.

"I wasn't sure I was going to make it. There was a long line at the rest room. Glad you saved me a seat."

"Those boys wanted me to sit with them," I whisper.

"No, you stay with me, I'll get you to LA and we'll talk along the way. It's a long trip so we can try to pass the time getting to know each other better," Patty smiles.

"Who was the man in the sunglasses? Is he going to be on our bus?'

Once again Patty hesitates before she answers me, "Oh, he just asked me about some directions. I told him I'm not from San Diego and I couldn't help him. Who knows what he was up to."

Relief sweeps over me like a cool breeze as I sit next to Patty for the rest of the trip to Los Angeles. Patty explains the normal trip by car would be about two and half hours, but by bus we'll be lucky to get there in three hours. If there's traffic it could take us four hours.

Patty shares some pastries she bought and I am happy to save the sandwiches for later. She glances at her phone with a frightened look on her face while eating the pastries.

"Is there something wrong Patty? You look worried," I say with concern.

"I've texted my boyfriend at least four times and he hasn't answered. On my phone it says he received the message. I'm not sure why he doesn't answer me," Patty says.

"He must be at work. If he is working he can't answer you right now. Don't worry. He will answer soon," I reassure her.

"I hope so, I don't know another person in LA besides him. I shouldn't try to surprise him. I should call him to see if he answers. Why don't you tell me a little about your family if you can. It might help you the more you talk about it," Patty says.

"Sometimes when I'm distracted I forget why I am going to Oregon. I'll tell you but it may take me a few minutes to get the whole story out. But I guess we have time."

"Take your time."

"A few weeks ago my family went to San Felipe, it's a village in Baja, California. We went to visit my father's sister Elena. Every summer we go to San Felipe to visit for a long weekend. My brother, sister and I love to go to the beach there. My mom and dad get to visit friends and family and we all enjoy some time away from the ranchito. You see, we live on a ranchito three hours out of town. We only go when my father can get some free time. He works for the Gutierrez family and doesn't like to leave the work to them while he is gone."

Patty hands me another pastry and says, "Go on."

"I asked permission to stay an extra week in San Felipe. I have some friends there and there are dances. Where we live there aren't many young people besides the owner's son. I wish now that I never asked to stay in town. My father gave me permission because he also wanted me to help out my Tía Elena. She has some disabilities and needs extra help sometimes."

I pause and look out the window, "We got the news on Saturday morning, there had been an accident. The police came to Tía Elena's house. They told us that my family had died in a car accident on the highway about ten kilometers from the ranchito."

"Oh Sara, I'm so sorry. How horrible for you," Patty says as she takes my hand in her own.

"I thought that was the worst news I would ever get, and things couldn't get worse. But they did get worse. My Tía Elena began to say she needed more money to help pay rent and buy groceries. My dad always paid her rent and helped buy groceries because she could only work part time and didn't earn a lot of money. I didn't know how much he helped her until she told me she couldn't pay the rent with her salary. I told her I would get a job and help out. I'm seventeen and I could get a job someplace in San Felipe to help pay rent."

"That must be difficult but it makes sense you would help her out. So, what happened?" Patty asks.

"My primo Juan started coming to the house and telling my Tía Elena that she should send me to Oregon with my other uncle.

If she did that there wouldn't be any problems. At first my Tía Elena said no, it would be impossible to send me away. She needed me with her. But, I noticed each time that Juan left she would give him some money. It made me angry because Juan is young and able to work. He shouldn't take money from her. She later explained that it was protection money. She needed to give him money so the narcos wouldn't bother us. That made me angrier. Because of me she had to give them more money. You see, the narcos run the small villages in Mexico and the people are very afraid. If they ask for money most people pay them. I don't think my father knew this was happening. If he knew he would have taken my Tía Elena to the ranchito with us."

"So you have to earn money to protect your Tía?" Patty asks.

"Yes, to protect her and also help her with rent, medicines and groceries. My primo Juan won't help her. I'm the only one left to help. I don't want to go to Oregon, but I have to go. My uncle in Oregon isn't a nice person. My father never liked him and we didn't have a lot of contact with him. Now, I have to go live with him and hope he will help me find a job. He told my Tía that he doesn't owe me anything, why should he take me in?"

"That is so sad, Sara. I hope things get better for you soon," Patty says as her phone beeps. She looks down at her phone and smiles. Her boyfriend sent her a text. He will meet her at the bus station when she arrives.

"At least he'll pick me up. I don't know what will happen when he sees my pregnant belly," She laughs.

"You are lucky someone who loves you is waiting for you. I would be very happy if when I got off the bus in Oregon there was a boyfriend waiting for me or anyone that is happy to see me."

"Sara, listen to me. If things don't work out in Oregon you call me. I will help you. I know I will need help with daycare, you could come to be my nanny. Go see your uncle and if he is mean or rude to you, call me right away," Patty offers.

It surprises me to hear Patty's offer, "That is so nice Patty. You are so kind. I'm so relieved I met you at the bus station."

Patty reaches in her purse to find a pencil and paper. She scribbles her name and number on a card, then hands it to me.

"I put my number and my boyfriend's number. You can call either one if you need help. I won't forgive myself if anything happens to you."

Chapter 6

As the greyhound approaches LA. I am amazed at the amount of traffic. I'm not used to such a large city with so many cars. I realize my trip has been easier because of Patty. I would be so unsure of everything if I hadn't talked with Patty during the long bus ride. She has been so patient with my imperfect English. Patty is asleep with her head tilted back and mouth open. I worry about her, and about myself. I have no idea what awaits me in Oregon. Will my uncle's family accept me? Will they be kind? What kind of living situation will it be? I know I have two cousins, one my own age. Will I share a room? I hope I will get my own bed and some privacy. What if I only have a place to sleep on the sofa or even on the floor? What if my uncle lives in a neighborhood with gangs or a lot of crime? What if he is mean to me? What if the gangs in Oregon are as bad as the ones in the border towns in Mexico? Anxiety takes over my body and mind, and perspiration drips down my forehead and the back of my neck. Things start to get blurry and I feel sick. What should I do? Should I sit and wait for it to pass or get up and try to make it to the toilet in the back of the bus?

"Sara, what's wrong? Can you hear me?" Patty pats me on my leg.

"Sara, talk to me. Are you okay?" Again Patty touches me trying to get me to snap out of my trance.

"What? Oh, I'm hot and dizzy. Things start to get blurry. I feel like I'm going to be sick. Give me a minute and if I keep my eyes closed maybe it will pass," I respond.

"Here, drink some water," Patty says as she hands the plastic bottle to me.

I take small sips from the bottle with my eyes closed. Patty takes out a tissue from her purse and starts wiping the sweat from my forehead.

"Sara, do you feel better?"

"Yes, I don't know what happened. This has never happened before."

"It could be a panic attack. I've seen it before. Do you get all hot and feel like you can't move? Like you can hardly breathe? You might be sick, but I think it's a panic attack. After all you have been through it wouldn't surprise me. You need to take care of yourself," Patty pats my hand.

"Thanks Patty. I start to worry about what it will be like in Oregon and how my uncle will treat me. I don't even know if I have a place to sleep. What happens if they don't pick me up at the bus station? What will I do then?" I cry.

"Remember, you are going to call me. You have my number. If he doesn't pick you up you call me right away. We'll figure something out, okay?"

"Thanks, that helps me to know I can call you," I whisper.

"We have about fifty miles to go, we should eat something, food always helps me relax." Patty says.

"I don't know if I can eat. I'm nauseous. But I'll try to drink a juice."

"Good, I'll take out a sandwich and open it up, if it's in front of you, you might decide to take a bite," Patty encourages.

"Okay, that's a good idea. Let's share a sandwich. I am a little hungry. How about some of those chips? Sometimes salt helps me settle my stomach."

Patty reaches in her bag for chips.

"Here we can spread it all out on my purse." Patty says as she puts her purse on the arm rest between the two of us. As she does it, I notice a small handgun in her purse. Why would she carry a gun? Is it for protection or should I be afraid of her. I look at her as she hands me half of a sandwich. She doesn't look dangerous. I think I can trust her. I heard everyone carries a gun here.

"I am starting to feel better," I tell her. "I need to remember to eat and drink. That police officer tricked me. I don't know who to trust any more."

"No he wasn't a nice person, you need to be very careful. If you are lucky you won't meet any more people like him. You know he wasn't a police officer, right?"

I turn to look at Patty, "Yes, I know he wasn't a police officer. But, please don't ever say I am lucky."

"I'm sorry, Sara. I know things aren't easy."

I chew my sandwich and look away. I don't feel lucky and it angers me to think others think so. My life has become a nightmare from morning til night. My grief is overwhelming, sometimes I can't even think. The only time I can relax is when I am able to distract myself and think about other things, but it doesn't last long..

We are getting closer to the exit for Los Angeles. I watch as others start to sit up and gather their things. Many people slept on the trip from San Diego. In a few minutes I will be alone again. Patty will leave and meet up with her boyfriend and I'll be alone. I hope she'll help me find my bus.

We cross a bridge over a highway and soon we are on another one just as wide. The roads and highways here in Los Angeles are so big. There are so many cars and they drive so fast here. Our bus blends in with the traffic and we head west and I see the sun is setting. Some tall buildings in the distance are silhouetted in the sun, I realize Los Angeles is bigger than I expected. The skyscrapers tower above the city and look so uninviting. I never wanted to visit Los Angeles, but here I am. Another first for me, so many firsts for me.

The traffic is stop and go, but our bus driver seems to be able to navigate through the lanes of traffic to keep us moving. Soon we are exiting the highway and turning on to a city street.

"We're almost here!" Patty exclaims.

"Yes, almost here. But I have an even longer distance to go on another bus."

Patty looks over at me with pity in her eyes. I wonder what she is thinking. She is about to give birth and start a new life here in LA and I have no idea what awaits me in my future. I feel so alone.

On the left I see many buses, we slow down and pull in to the parking area. The driver speaks into his microphone and says, "LA folks. Last stop for this bus. Gather your belongings and exit the bus when we stop. This bus does not continue on today."

While on the bus I don't need to make any decisions or worry about my uncle. The bus is like a cocoon that holds me safely as it rolls down the highway. Now I need to exit my cocoon and hope to find another one that feels as safe. Patty looks out the window and waves. Her boyfriend is standing on the sidewalk waiting for her. He is tall, dressed in dark clothes and wears dark reflective sunglasses and a baseball cap pulled down over his glasses. He smiles and waves back. He looks like he is trying to hide from someone.

I pick up my backpack and stand up. It's time to move, time to step off the bus and hope no one else tries to kidnap me. I want to stay close to Patty but know she will leave with her boyfriend. Until she does I'm going to stay very close to her. As Patty walks down the aisle of the bus her sunglasses drop to the floor from her bag. I lean down and pick them up, the glasses look expensive. So many people wear sunglasses here I may need these and I slip them in my pocket, she doesn't even notice.

We get off the bus and Patty waddles over to her boyfriend who laughs when he sees her pregnant belly. He hugs her in a friendly manner rather than a loving manner. Maybe he isn't as excited about the baby as she is. They talk quietly before calling me over.

"John, this is Sara. She is traveling alone, we got to know each other on the bus."

John held out his hand to me and said, "Nice to meet you. Glad Patty didn't have to sit alone on the bus. If I had known I would have driven down to pick her up. But she surprised me with the visit and this," he points at her large baby bump.

"I'm glad you didn't because I enjoyed talking with Sara. It was a long trip but she is now a friend for life. She's been through a lot. I told her to call us if she has any problems, right Sara?"

Yes, I will call you. Don't worry. I will call you as soon as I have access to a phone in Woodburn. Thanks again for your help."

"Let's help you find your bus to Oregon. Do you have your ticket? It looks like you have thirty minutes before your bus leaves."

"Yes, it's here. Los Angeles to Portland, I guess Portland must be near Woodburn. I hope my uncle will be there," I start to worry again.

"Remember to look for friendly people. If you have a question look for an employee at the bus station. Please don't leave with anyone who tries to help you. You look a little lost and people may try to take advantage," Patty says as she folds me in to a hug.

"I know, I'll be careful. I wish you could come with me. I'll call to let you know when I arrive and also to find out about your baby. Best of luck with your baby."

"Thanks, get on the bus before I cry. Get on the bus." Patty pushes me toward the door of the bus, a second time someone pushes me to get in to a vehicle.

I don't turn around. I walk to the back of the bus and step up to the last leg of my trip. The Greyhound will make ten stops along the twenty-one hour trip. I know it will be a long trip, but I hope I will feel safe in a my cocoon again. I don't have to get off the bus until I arrive at my destination. I look around to see the other passengers settle in for the long trip. Some talk while others sit with eyes closed and earbuds in their ears. I don't have a book or a device to listen to music. I pull out my notebook and start a letter to Tía Elena.

Querida Tía,

I am now safe and across the border. I made a new friend in the bus station in Caléxico. We sat together all the way from Caléxico to Los Angeles. I hated to say goodbye to her in Los Angeles but that was her destination. She helped me pass the time and not worry too much. Tía, I never knew I had to be so careful.

The bus ride from LA to Woodburn is twenty-one hours long. The bus will stop along the way, but I don't need to change buses. I will mail this as soon as I have a stamp.

Te echo de menos, Tía, I wish you could be here with me. You would know what to do. You would make me feel safe.

The border crossing was confusing but not as scary as I thought. I hope to never see that family again. Do you know they make their children lie and cause problems to help them pass over the border? They cause confusion and the guards look like they never want to see them again and wave them through. As soon as we were across they stopped being friendly to me. They dropped me at the bus station in Caléxico and left before I even knew what bus I needed. They told me they don't make extra money helping people after they cross the border. I never knew there were people so hateful, Tía. While I lived in Baja everyone was nice and I didn't have to be careful. From now on I need to take care of myself. I will send you some money as soon as I can.

Besos y un abrazo muy grande,
Sarita

Chapter 7

I stay awake during the stops in California. When we get to Sacramento most of the passengers get off. I wonder why so many people want to go to Sacramento, is it a nice place to live? Soon the bus is empty and the driver stands up and looks back at me.

"You aren't getting off? We have thirty minutes here, you might want to get out and walk around."

"No thanks. Does this bus go to Oregon?" I ask.

"What, I can't hear you. Could you say it again? Do you speak Spanish?" The driver asks.

"Yes, I speak Spanish. Does this bus goes to Oregon?" I try to make my question easier to understand. I realize I need to repeat myself sometimes for people to understand. I want to speak as much English as possible.

"Yep. We leave in thirty minutes. I have to lock the bus, are you staying?" He asks.

"Yes, I will stay here until we leave."

"Whatever you want young lady. No one can get on until I come back so you are safe here. Sit back and close your eyes," The driver says as he steps off the bus and locks the door.

I lean back and relax for the second time since I left San Felipe. It's like a sudden flash of lightening in my head when I realize I am alone in a quiet safe place. It's dark but I can see everything outside of the bus. People walk around with cups of coffee and food. It looks like they want to spend as much time off the bus as possible. I see a man standing near the coffee stand, he is staring at me. He turns and looks away when he sees me looking at him. Is that John? Is that Patty's boyfriend? It can't be, why is he here? Maybe because I'm tired everyone starts to look alike.

The tears run down my cheeks. I try not to think about everything that happened in the past week. Now the quiet of the bus overwhelms me. I start to feel very sleepy. Everything happened so quick. One minute I was spending my vacation in San Felipe with my family and the next I was living with Tía Elena.

Now, undocumented and in a place where I don't know anyone, I'm alone. I know my uncle is not happy to have me live with his family. How can things change so much in such a short time? How I wish I could change things.

I rest my eyes and try to wrangle the thoughts in my head. The idea of being on my own is terrifying. My thoughts return to earlier today. Was it only this morning I left San Felipe? I find it so hard to believe. The next thing I hear is the click of the lock on the door. The driver is back and the other passengers get on the bus as soon as he sat in his seat. I see the line of people getting on the bus. I hope I can keep the seat next to me empty. I also notice many of the passengers are Spanish speaking. I recognize some as my countrymen by their speech, but others are Guatemalan. Why are so many Mexicans and Guatemalans going to Oregon? I wonder if it is true that there is a lot of work in Oregon. I hope so. Then I can send Tía Elena money and pay off the coyote.

A young mother with her baby asks to sit next to me. I smile and motion for the woman to sit. At least I won't have to worry about the young men on the bus. If they ask to sit next to me I wouldn't be able to relax or sleep. If this young mother gets her baby to sleep we can all sleep. It's already 2:30 a.m.

The bus pulls out of the bus station and people start to quiet down. Most want to sleep for the rest of the trip. The woman next to me speaks Spanish and says she wants to sleep as long as her baby is asleep. This makes me happy because I feel safe and protected while the woman is next to me.

I drift off to sleep with my head against the window. I don't wake until the bus pulls in to a town called Weed. I look around, the baby next to me wakes up and smiles. Her mother still sleeps so I play a game of peekaboo with the baby. The giggling wakes the mother up. She looks at me and smiles.

"Thank you. I was able to sleep. It is a long trip with a baby."

"Would you like me to hold her so you can stand up and move around?" I offer.

"Yes, thanks," she hands me the baby and stands up.

"Do you mind if I get down to grab a coffee? I can bring you one too. You can hold her until I get back," The mother seems too eager to leave the baby with me.

"Sure, go ahead. I can watch her. Could you get me a coffee with milk and sugar please?" I reach in to my pocket to get money.

"No, don't worry. I've got this," The young mom walks down the aisle and gets off. She hurries toward the coffee truck parked outside the bus station. I watch her and wonder how old this young woman is. She seems very young. Few mothers would leave their babies with a total stranger to get a cup of coffee. The baby starts to cry and I bounce her up and down trying to calm her down.

So far I've made friends with Patty and now with the young mother and baby. The trip that started out so emotional is turning in to an adventure. I think the adventure could be interesting if it wasn't due to tragic circumstances. The mother returns with two cups of coffee and two sweet breads.

"Here, I thought you might like a bear claw with your coffee. They are sweet but taste so good."

"What are they called? Bear claus? Like Santa Claus?" I ask.

"No, like the big paw of a bear," she explains as she holds up her hand in the shape of a big paw.

"Oh, I get it. Like the hand of a bear." I laugh. I can't believe I can laugh over such a silly thing as a sweet roll.

The hot coffee and bear claw tastes so good. The sweet, sugary topping on the bear claw helps settle my stomach. It will help me sleep well on the trip and I don't realize I am hungry. I've met people and also learned about the food. This adventure is very interesting.

The bus starts up and people chat, soon we pass the Welcome to Oregon sign and I sigh. I made it to Oregon, now what can be next for me?

Chapter 8

The bus stops in Medford, Grants Pass, Eugene and finally Salem. The woman and baby get off in Eugene and I hope I can have the seat next to me empty until I get off in Woodburn. I sit alone until we get to Salem.

Sitting on the bus in Salem I look up and see a young man coming toward my seat. I hope he sits behind me and not next to me. I look away and he sits in the seat behind me. That was close, I don't feel like telling anyone else my story and people seem so nosey.

A young couple get on the bus and look around for two empty seats. There aren't any two seats together. I hope they don't ask me to move, I don't want to move. They whisper something to each other and look right at me. Oh no, they are going to ask me to move.

The young woman starts to ask me a question, but the man behind me gets up and sits with me before she can finish her sentence. I look over at him thankful I don't have to move, but also hesitant to speak to him. The couple sits in the seat behind us.

"I think it's easier if I sit with you. You don't have to move. How far are you going?"

"Woodburn, I'm going to Woodburn."

"Oh, that's not far. We"ll be there in a few minutes." He says and closes his eyes behind his sunglasses.

I remember Patty's sunglasses in my bag. Glad I picked them up, it seems like so many people here wear sunglasses. As the bus pulls on to I-5 in Salem I see a sign for Woodburn. The big green sign on the highway says Woodburn 19, Portland 47.

Is it possible my trip is almost over? The inside of this bus had been my home for the past two days. The bus helps me to feel safe because I don't have to make any decisions. When I arrive in Woodburn I will have to meet my uncle and family and try to fit in. I hope they will welcome me and make me feel safe in their home.

The bus slows and pulls in to a parking lot near Taco Bell and Walmart. It circles through both parking lots and stops in front of a mini mart.

In the window I see a sign that says: Greyhound stops here. There are a few cars parked in front of the store.

I stand up when the driver yells out, "Woodburn, next stop Portland."

I walk down the aisle of the bus with other passengers. Some grab suitcases from the rack above their seat while others carry backpacks. Each waits while the others gather their things. When I step off the bus I don't see anyone waiting for me. I look around to see if someone who resembles my dad is there waiting. But no, no one is here to pick me up. The bus leaves me standing alone in a cloud of exhaust. I cough and try not to cry. Now what? What if my uncle doesn't come to get me? What will I do? I don't know anyone here. I don't even know my uncle. As the tears start to blind me I hear a car drive up.

"Sara? Are you Sara? Soy tu tío. Jump in. I'm late and I need to pick up my daughter. Hurry up," Tío Enrique says.

I jump in to the passenger side of a white Ford Explorer. The car is already in gear and pulling out of the parking lot before I could close the door. I try to put on my seat belt. A cloud of silence hung in the vehicle like fog. He doesn't say anything for five minutes but keeps looking over at me.

"You look like your mother," he snarls.

"People tell me that," I say.

"You'll have to move to the back seat when I pick up my daughter."

"Okay, I can do that, Tío Enrique ..." I start to say but he cuts me off.

"I don't want to hear any arguing, you hear me. I am taking you in but not because I want to, it's because you don't have anyone else. You'll share a room with your cousin and on Monday I'll start looking for a job for you. There is a job with Fish Camp but it doesn't start right away," he says as the car slows.

"What is Fish Camp?" I ask.

"It's a job you can get, one of the few jobs unless you want to work in the fields. Do you want to work in the fields?" Tío Enrique asks.

"No, I can get the job at the Fish camp," I answer.

"Please don't get comfortable at our house and don't distract my daughter. She is very intelligent and plans to be a doctor. We don't need you bringing her down with your drama or tragic stories. She doesn't need to hear it—do you understand me?" Tío Enrique glares at me.

The Explorer slows and pulls in to the high school parking lot. As Enrique drives up to the entrance he flashes the lights at his daughter. A young girl with long dark hair turns and waves. "That's your cousin Natalia, remember what I told you."

"Hola, hija. How was your day?" Enrique leans over and gives his daughter a kiss on the cheek.

"Fine," Natalia slides into the front seat and turns around and smiles.

"Are you my cousin, Sara? I never knew I had a cousin the same age. Nice to meet you, Bienvenida. Will you be staying with us?" Natalia says as she reaches out to me with her hand.

I blush and a feeling of absolute loneliness engulfs me. Natalia doesn't even know I exist and now she doesn't know I will be living with them. The panic starts to set in again. Beads of sweat run down the back of my neck and I have the urge to vomit. I try to speak but the words won't come out. I close my eyes and try to relax.

"Papá, something is wrong with Sara. She looks like she is going to be sick. Pull over," Natalia says. She opens her door as soon as the car stops and runs to open the back door.

"Sara, here let me help you. ¿Qué te pasa?" Natalia reaches to help me get out of the back seat.

"I am a little nauseous, let me walk a little. I've been on the bus for two days and I need to walk and get some fresh air."

"Okay, I'll walk with you. I'll tell my dad."

"Papá, I'm going to walk with Sara a little bit. Meet us over there by Dutch Brothers Coffee. She needs some fresh air," Natalia waves for her father to drive away.

"I know things have been difficult for you. I was so sad when I heard about your family. But you are here now and we will take care of you. Let's walk," Natalia said as she put her arm around my shoulder.

I realize Natalia doesn't know what her father said. He won't let her see how cruel he can be. I'll need to stay as close to Natalia as possible to escape the wrath of Tío Enrique.

"Thanks Natalia, I'm glad you're here with me. I need a friend."

"I'm not your friend I'm your cousin. We're family. Family takes care of each other. I never knew about you until yesterday. My dad never told me. He doesn't talk much about his childhood. He is so proud of the work he's done here to make a nice home for us. Now, it'll be your home too. Let's go so we can get home for dinner. My mom will have dinner waiting, she will be so happy to see you," Natalia says as we hurry to the waiting vehicle.

Before I could get in to the back seat Natalia pushes me out of the way and says, "No, you sit up front if you are nauseous. I'm fine, I'll sit in the back," Natalia holds the front door open for me. I notice my uncle give me a mean look, but I step up in to the Explorer and close the door.

"Papá, why didn't you tell me before I had a cousin my age in Mexico? I never knew until yesterday. Why did you keep it a secret?" Natalia asks.

"Natalia, let's talk about it later, okay?" Tío Enrique says as he drives out of the parking lot on to the highway.

Natalia continues to ask her father questions.

"Are you embarrassed of your roots, Papá? You know we look Mexican no matter where we live, right? There is no way you can denounce your heritage, you should be proud of it. I don't get why you never told us."

"Enough! All right? We'll talk later," Enrique ends the conversation by raising his hand in the air and hitting the steering wheel. The car starts to speed up and I realize my uncle has a temper. I will need to be careful. I decide I will try to never be alone with Tío Enrique.

Chapter 9

The Explorer turns off the highway and enters into a neighborhood of large homes with manicured lawns. It's obvious this is a nice area with expensive homes. I look at each house as we pass by. It seems like all of the homes have at least two cars parked in the driveway and sometimes more. Tío Enrique and his family live here? Does he have a lot of money? I didn't expect his house to be so nice.

We pull in to the driveway of a large white house with blue shutters. On the front porch hang two baskets of bright-red geraniums. The lights on either side of the door are lit and the house looks very welcoming. Although the house looks very homey I get the same treatment I got from my uncle from Enrique's wife Karina, cold and hateful. It's obvious she doesn't agree with the idea of me living with them. Karina hugs Natalia as we enter the house but she holds out her hand to me. No welcoming hugs for me.

"Natalia, show Sara to your room. We put a cot in your room. She can sleep with you"

"A cot? We have an extra bed in the basement. There's lots of space in my room for another bed. Can we bring up the bed tomorrow? I want Sara to be comfortable," Natalia says.

"She's here to work, not to be comfortable. Your father thinks he found her some work so she won't be here long. Fish Camp is hiring and if she goes to work there she will sleep there," Karina says.

"She just got here Mamá. She should be comfortable in our house. When my other cousin comes over you go out of your way to make everyone comfortable, even making me sleep on the sofa. Why is it different with Sara?" Natalia cries.

"Come on Sara, I'll show you our room. You can sleep in my bed tonight. I'll sleep in the cot," Natalia says as she leads me up the stairs.

"Oh no, Natalia I don't want to cause any problems. Please, I'll sleep in the little bed or what do you call it, a cot? It's not a problem," I say as I put my backpack down on the smallest bed in the room.

"I don't know why my parents are acting like this. I knew my father had a brother in Baja but he never talked about him or about his family. Do you know why?"

"No, I don't. My father didn't speak of your family either. We knew he had a brother he hadn't spoken with for a long time. Do you know about Tía Elena? She is your father's disabled sister who lives alone in San Felipe. I am here because I need to help her pay bills and rent. She doesn't make enough money to pay for everything on her own. My father always helped her out, and now that he's gone it's my job. I never expected to have to start work so young or move to a new country. This is all so overwhelming for me. I'm so happy you are my cousin, Natalia."

"Me too, Sara. I didn't know anything about Tía Elena. I wonder why my father is so secretive."

Karina calls to Natalia, "Come down to dinner. We are all waiting for you two."

"On our way, Mamá. Let's go, Sara. My brother is home and they won't pay much attention to us if he is at the dinner table. Watch how many times my father asks him a question and then how many times he talks with me. It's such a joke. We'll eat quick and come back upstairs. Come on," Natalia takes my hand and pulls me down the stairs.

"Milagro." Natalia's brother, Jose says. I look over to see a tall, thin young man with huge brown eyes and lots of long, curly black hair. I gasp and my face turns red.

"What's wrong, Sara?" Natalia asks.

"I know what's wrong," Tío Enrique answers.

"Sit down you two," Karina snaps.

"He looks so much like my father, the same hair and eyes. He's tall like my father and it surprises me, that's all. It's a shock," I explain.

Karina gets up and leaves the table without a comment. She fumbles around in the kitchen looking for a serving spoon. When she comes back to the table everyone is quiet and I hide my eyes by looking down.

"Okay, the shock is over. José looks like his uncle, let's eat before the dinner gets cold," Karina says.

I hardly taste the food. I eat it and swallow it as quickly as possible. I only want this dinner to be over. I watch as Enrique chatters with José about sports and José's girlfriend. Natalia kicks me under the table each time the conversation focuses on José. I notice Enrique and Karina ask Natalia two questions through the whole dinner.

Neither one bothers to ask me about my trip, my family, the accident or if I want more food. It's obvious that my stay here will not be pleasant. I hope the job at Fish Camp starts soon. It will be better than staying here as an unwanted guest.

CHAPTER 10

The following day Natalia, José, Karina and Enrique all leave the house at eight am. Karina gives me a list of things to do in the house while they are gone, with no please or thank you. The list includes cleaning the house, making dinner and doing laundry. I hope I can get it all finished before they return.

Enrique and Karina's room is the largest in the house and is decorated in the style of La Pulga, or flea market. That's the first room to clean. The frilly curtains and lampshades with lace are all items I've seen in the flea market in San Felipe. The style must have come across the border with Karina when she moved to Oregon. You can take the girl out of Mexico, but you can't take Mexico out of the girl. My mom had less money and better taste.

Next is José's dark room, all the shades are drawn and no natural light enters in to this cavern. I'm almost afraid to turn the light on, I'll come back and vacuum later. The clothes on the floor is where I begin to gather the laundry. A basket is filled from José's room alone. The laundry room is off the kitchen and the washer is complicated but I figure out the instructions in English. The first load is José's clothes, how can one person have this many pairs of jeans? I start the machine, add soap and close the lid. I look around for the vacuum. After a short search I find it in the hall closet. I plug it in and start to clean the carpet in the living room and dining room. I move with the vacuum up the stairs to finish the bedrooms. I find cleaning supplies for the bathrooms under the sink and finish the upstairs bathrooms. In the next hour I clean the whole house and leave it shining.

When I hear the washer signal the end of the load, I move the laundry from the washer to the dryer. I bring more clothes from Tío Enrique and Karina's room and start the next load. I reach in Tío Enrique's pocket and find a small empty plastic bag. It looks like white sugar in in the bottom of the bag. I put the bag in a tray on top of the washer and reach in to the other pocket. Inside the pocket is a crumpled piece of paper with names with amounts of money next to them. I leave the paper in the tray too.

Back in the kitchen I look in the cupboards to see what I can make for dinner. I still have half a day left and there is time to make a homemade dinner. In the pantry there are some pinto beans and rice. If I want to make beans I need to get them started. I pull out an olla and pour the frijoles into the pan and fill it with water. I wash them and rinse them as my mom taught me. I refill the pot with water, add salt, garlic an onion and I put the beans on to cook. The cooked frijoles will be tasty.

In the refrigerator tomatoes, jalapeños and lettuce wait to be made into salsa and a salad. The salsa reminds me of Tía Elena and I remember I have to send her letter. The salsa will be perfect because she taught me how to make it. In the fridge I also see Don Pancho tortillas in a plastic bag.

They look nothing like the tortillas my mother used to make. Sadness starts to creep in and I push it back with all my might, I can't start thinking about my family. I have a warm place to sleep, food and someone who will help me find a job. I can't fall in the habit of letting my grief take over my life. My hair falls in my eyes and I push it back and sigh. Homemade tortillas won't take long, all the ingredients are in the pantry and there is plenty of time. I look over to see a TV in the corner of the kitchen. The remote is on the counter and I click the power button to turn it on, it will keep me company while I make the tortillas. I scan the channels and find a cooking show and decide it will help me learn more English.

The time flies by. The frijoles are almost ready. The tortillas are ready to put on the plancha. The salad is made, the salsa too and all I need to do is set the table. I start to worry. What if they don't like my food? What if they want hamburgers or hot dogs? What if I used too many ingredients? Will Karina get mad at me? I'll have to wait and see. If they don't like it I'm sure they'll tell me.

The laundry washed, dried and folded is on top of the dryer. I don't dare try to put it away because I don't want to look in the dresser drawers or closets unless they ask me to. I look around and am satisfied everything is clean, dinner is made and the laundry is finished. I hope they appreciate my hard work, or at least let me stay without too many problems.

Karina comes home first, she says hello as she enters the house but nothing more. When she comes into the kitchen she sees the dinner is ready to finish. She frowns and looks around.

"You've been busy haven't you? Did you vacuum upstairs?"

"Yes, and I brought down laundry. The folded laundry is on top of the washer," I answer.

"What did you make for dinner besides tortillas and beans? Did you make chicken?" Karina asks.

"No, I didn't know how much food to make. I thought beans, tortillas, rice and salad would be enough," I explain.

"In this house we have meat or chicken for every dinner. We aren't poor like in Mexico. We can afford to buy meat for every dinner. I'll get the chicken ready," Karina says.

"I can do it, if you want. You go rest, you've been working all day. Please, I can do it. Do you want it roasted or fried?" I ask.

"Broiled, there is a broiler in the oven. Turn this switch here, you put the chicken on a tray and keep turning it. It should cook in twenty minutes. In the meantime I'm going upstairs. Can you have this done by six?" Karina asks.

"Yes, of course. It will cook by six. Don't worry."

Enrique, Natalia and José arrive home at 5:45. Karina comes downstairs and greets all three. A waft of shower gel and shampoo fills the air. She is refreshed with a cute outfit, and a made-up face.

"Hi everyone. Dinner is almost ready, get washed up and we'll eat right away."

"Wow, that's great. We don't have to wait while you cook. We should have hired a maid earlier," Tío Enrique says in English.

I overhear the comment about the maid. I think I understand what it means, but I'm not sure. Does he mean I am a servant in their house? Did he call me a maid? My mind wanders to a place where I see myself as a servant living with my own family until I'm eighty years old. What kind of future awaits me here in the United States? I don't mind doing the work and I love helping out, but if they consider me a maid it means I'm not family. It means I'll be an orphan forever, they won't treat me as their niece, only a servant. I hope I misunderstood my uncle.

"Sara, bring the food to the table. It must be ready now," Karina says as she sits down in her chair at the table like a queen waiting for her butlers to serve dinner.

"Okay, I'm serving it on platters now. It'll be a minute," I answer.

Natalia gets up and starts to go to the kitchen to help me. Karina motions for her to sit down and wait.

"Mamá, I'm going to help Sara bring the food. Why should she serve us? She's a guest in our house. I'm going to help," Natalia answers.

"Sit down Natalia." Tío Enrique raises his voice.

"Papá! Why are you acting like this?" Natalia says as she sits back down in her seat.

"While Sara is here she will be cleaning, cooking and doing laundry. Your mother needs a break after working all day. I want her to rest and relax. I've never been able to pay anyone to help out, but since Sara is here she can do it," Tío Enrique explains.

"Did you ask her? Or do you expect her to do it and you won't say anything to her?" Natalia snaps at her father.

"Natalia, I don't mind. I can help out. Your papá is right, your Mamá can use the rest," I say as I carry the food to the table.

CHAPTER 11

Last night Natalia told me how hard it had been for her mother and father when they first arrived in the States. Natalia says she loves the new house, but worries about her mother and father.

When Karina first moved here with Tío Enrique they started out at low-waged jobs. They lived in a small apartment with another family and never seemed to earn enough money. They scraped by each paycheck. Two years ago Tío Enrique started driving a delivery truck and earning a lot more money.

They were able to move out of their small apartment and move into a nicer neighborhood. Karina wasn't sure how they could afford the house, but Tío Enrique assured her his new job would help them make the payments. It was too good to be true and she knew it. She agreed to move to the new house if he promised she wouldn't have to work two jobs. Karina continued to work five shifts a week at the hospital. Tío Enrique started to work long hours on his delivery job. The mortgage payments were always on time and Karina never even knew how much they paid each month. As long as her family could live in a nice house on a nice street she was content. At times she worried the happiness would be short-lived, but she learned to push the worries away. Now that Sara was here she would have everything done at home and there would be no worries.

Natalia also told me Karina is always tired when she arrives home from work and never has time to make a homemade dinner. Her job as a nurse's aide at the hospital is exhausting. Karina works to help pay for their big American-style home. She wants her children to have the best, better than what she had when she lived in Mexico. Her family was from Loreto, there never was a lot of money growing up. She hates her job but loves the idea that her children live in a nice American house and don't worry about money. Their lives are better.

José fills his plate and smiles, "This is great, Sara. Homemade tortillas and everything. When is the last time you made homemade tortillas, Mamá?"

Karina's face reddens and José looks like he regrets what he said, "Sorry, Mamá. I didn't mean anything. I know how hard you work and how tired you are."

"Sara, could you bring more salsa?" Karina snaps.

"Yes, sure." I stand up and and go to the kitchen.

"Mamá, she isn't a servant. I can get the salsa," Natalia says.

"Sit down Natalia," her father orders once again.

I return with more salsa and another platter with chicken and rice.

"Here, I kept this warm on the stove," I say as I place the platter on the table.

"Sit down Sara," Enrique says. "I called today to see if they have a place for you at Fish Camp. "

Karina stops eating and looks up, "What? Already? She just started helping us here at the house. I thought we agreed she would help us out for a while."

"I know, but they are leaving next week for Fish Camp. If we want her to go she will need to start next week. She can take care of the house until then," Tío Enrique explains.

Karina looks down at her plate and sighs.

"What is Fish Camp?" I ask. "What do you mean I have to leave? Where is Fish Camp?"

"It's on the coast. You'll be cleaning fish. They have an opening for six weeks. You will stay with them while you work," Tío Enrique explains.

"But I don't know anyone there, I only arrived yesterday. Now I have to leave? This is so hard. I promise I'll clean and cook for you every day. I'll make sure to finish the laundry. Please don't make me go away again," I plead.

Terror fills my heart once again. How much more can I take? So many demands and changes from everyone. I don't see others making sacrifices.

"This is part of the plan. You knew when Juan helped you get here you would have to work. Right? You knew we would help you get a job, but there were no guarantees you would get a job here and live with us," Tó Enrique says between bites of food.

"What? I didn't know I wouldn't be living here. I thought you were going to let me live here," I cry.

"Fish Camp starts next week. I'll tell them you'll be there," Tío Enrique says as he pushes his chair away from the table and stands up. "Until then you'll help around here."

"What if she goes to school with me? She could learn more English," Natalia says.

"She's not staying here, or going to school either. She's going to Fish Camp. That's the end of it," Tío Enrique says and walks away.

"Come Natalia, I need your help to finish a sewing project," Karina motions to her daughter.

"But Mamá, we need to clean up the dishes and the kitchen. Sara cooked dinner and spent all day cleaning. I'll help her first then come and help you."

"No, it's her job now to keep everything clean in the kitchen. At least for the time she is here. Don't argue, come upstairs and help me."

"I'll be there in a minute."

"Don't make me wait, I want to get a dress finished while Sara is here. I never have time to sew after dinner. Now I can. Hurry up."

"Okay, Mamá. I'll be right up." Karina left the room and went upstairs without saying a word to Sara.

"Sara, I am so embarrassed, I don't know why they are treating you this way. I've never seen my parents act like this before. I want to help you clean up," Natalia says as she helps clear the dishes from the table.

"Don't worry, I can take care of the dishes and the kitchen. What does everyone like for breakfast? I can also start preparing things for the morning."

"Breakfast? We usually grab a bagel and coffee on the way to school. My mom never has time to make breakfast. Don't worry."

"No, I'll make something. I'll take a look to see what is in the pantry and get it organized for tomorrow. Go ahead and go upstairs with your mother. I'll be fine."

"This is so awful, I hate how they are treating you!" Natalia says as she throws her hands in the air. She turns and leaves the room.

It's obvious now. They are going to treat me like a servant. Since they have made it so clear. I'll act like a maid to make them happy, If I can ever make them happy. No one finished their food. José ate more tortillas than anyone, but still left food on his plate. Should I make less or change what I make? Should I ask Karina? I can't handle all of this. I just got here, now I'm a servant but not for long because they are sending me away to clean fish on the coast. I don't even know how far away that is. Will I be able to come back and visit? Will they ever let me come back or will I be on my own once I leave?

I drop an empty pot on the floor. I am standing in the middle of the kitchen and I stare at a calendar on the wall. Notes on the calendar grab my attention. A week ago today my family was killed, the following date on the calendar says SARA. Sara what? Why would they write my name on the calendar the day after my family was killed? Was it to remind my Tío of my name? Had Tía Elena called him about the accident? That means they had made plans for me to come to Oregon even before the funeral. How could that be? I didn't know I was coming here until two days ago. I don't understand, why are things so confusing.

"Sara, what happened?" José asks.

"What? Oh, nothing. I mean ... José when did you know I was coming to your house?"

"A couple of days ago. Papá told me over the weekend. I didn't even know you existed until then. My father never mentioned your family. We knew there were some relatives in San Felipe, but we didn't know anything about you. I guess we have an aunt there too. Do you know her?"

"Yes, Tía Elena. She is your father's sister. That is why I'm here. I need to work to help her with her rent and other bills. She is handicapped. If your family helps her I wouldn't need to be here."

"Sara!" Tío Enrique snaps as he enters the kitchen.

"Didn't we talk about this? I don't want any drama or problems, remember? No more stories. I don't want my kids to hear about your family drama," Tío Enrique barks.

"I was asking about our Tía en San Felipe, it's not Sara's fault," José mumbles.

"No problem, hijo. Sara knows she doesn't need to talk about all of this with you, don't you Sara?"

"Yes. I know. It won't happen again."

"José, come and help me out in the garage. Let Sara finish up in here."

"Tío Enrique, what would you like for breakfast in the morning?" I ask.

"Huevos y tortillas. Café con leche. I leave the house at six tomorrow morning. Have it ready for me by 5:30," Tío Enrique says as he slams the kitchen door.

Five thirty in the morning, that's early. I need to get the ingredients out now to make the tortillas. I'll chop the jalapeños and make salsa tonight. There are some beans left from dinner, but I need to make more for tomorrow's dinner. I might as well get the beans started for tomorrow.

The date on the calendar is burned into my mind. I turn the lights off in the kitchen and walk upstairs to bed. Natalia is already asleep and I try to get ready for bed without waking her. I look around for an alarm clock and see one on the table next to my cot. I set the alarm for 4:45 and fall into bed. Sleep doesn't come for a couple of hours. I drift off to sleep with memories of the ranchito.

My dreams are cut short by the sound of the alarm. When I wake up I realize I'm not on the ranchito, I'm in Tío Enrique's house. I'm tired and afraid I'll do something wrong this morning. This is my second day here and I need to get up so I don't wake Natalia. I'll slip into the bathroom before anyone else and start the day with a hot shower. The shower is refreshing and helps me to wake up. I get dressed and head downstairs before Tío Enrique gets up, to get breakfast started.

Bacon, eggs and homemade tortillas are on the stove when I hear Tío Enrique come down the stairs. The coffee is brewed and the table set when Tío Enrique sits down at the table. He doesn't even say hello. He slurps his coffee and checks his phone. Will he ever treat me like a family member? Or at least be nice to me? I set the plate in front of him, homemade tortillas, crispy bacon, beans and scrambled eggs.

"No salsa?" he grunts.

"Yes, I'll bring it right away."

I set the small bowl of salsa next to his plate. He pours the entire bowl of salsa on his eggs and rolls the eggs and bean mixture up into a tortilla. The beans and salsa fall out of the tortilla but sounds of pleasure escape his mouth involuntarily. It's obvious he is enjoying his food. Maybe my cooking will make him be nicer to me. The way to a man's heart is through his stomach, I remember I learned in English class. I don't want him to love me, just be nicer to me. I'll settle for him talking to me in a kinder tone of voice. He continues to mumble while eating and more sounds of joy escape him. He really enjoys my food. A good start to the day.

Tío Enrique stands up, grabs his phone and wipes his mouth with the paper napkin.

"Tío Enrique, what would you like for dinner?"

"Carnitas, can you make carnitas?"

"Yes, but I think I need to buy some groceries. How do I do that?"

"Here is some money, the supermarket is a few blocks away. Walk there and get what you need. Clean up the house first. You have time to clean, do the laundry and get the groceries. Make sure you do what Karina asks you to do, understand?"

"Yes. Can you give me directions to the supermarket? I'm not sure I know where to go."

"It's on the highway. Go to the end of the street, turn left and walk another few blocks and you'll see the Safeway sign. It's a big supermarket."

He leaves without saying any more. I look down at the money he gave me. One hundred dollars, it seems like a lot of money but I have no idea how much things cost in the supermarket here. Karina and Natalia enter the room and sit down at the table. Natalia smiles and says good morning but Karina says nothing.

"Karina, what would you like for breakfast? I have eggs, bacon, frijoles and tortillas. Would you like me to bring you a plate?"

"No, just coffee and toast for me."

"I'll have some of the breakfast you cooked Sara," Natalia smiles.

"Okay, it'll be just a minute. How about José? Will he be eating breakfast?"

"He'll be down in a minute. Bring our food first, I have to get to work. Don't make me late," Karina says.

"Okay, I'll be right back. Tío Enrique asked me to make carnitas for dinner tonight. Is that okay with you?"

"He gave you money? How much did he give you?"

"One hundred dollars. He said to go to Safeway to buy what I needed. It's not far is it?"

"Safeway is far away, it will take you about twenty-five minutes to walk there. Why don't we drop you off on our way to school?" Natalia says.

"No, Natalia, Sara needs to finish the housework first. She has time to walk there and back. It will make us late to drop her off."

I set the food on the table for Karina and Natalia. As I finish giving them what they need José walks in and sits down.

"Huevos, tortillas and bacon for breakfast? Fantastic, I can get used to this."

"José, should I make you a plate?"

"Yes, please. It looks delicious. But I need to leave in five minutes, can you make it that quick?"

"It will be just a minute. Be right back."

If they come down to eat one by one every morning I will be serving breakfast from 5:30 to 8:00 every day. Why can't they all come down at the same time? I want to strangle Karina, but I need to be nice to her. Tío Enrique made it clear I need to follow everything she tells me. I will nod and smile if I can whenever she asks for something.

"Sara, your frijoles look a little dark. Are they completely cooked? Last night they tasted a bit burnt. You have to be very careful with frijoles you know."

"I didn't think they were burnt, " José says.

"Neither did I," Natalia chimes in.

"And today they are perfect. I love your frijoles Sara," José smiles.

"Karina, do you want me to change how I make them? How would you make them?"

José laughs then tries to stuff food in his mouth. Karina may not be a good cook, maybe José likes my food too much. I need to be careful. I don't want to cook bad food, but if my food is too good Karina is going to dislike me more.

"Just be careful. When you buy the pork for the carnitas look for a good price. Don't pay too much. Do you use Coke to make the carnitas? It helps keep them tender."

"I can do that. I can make them however you want."

"While you are at Safeway you can buy some rice, avocados and tomatoes. We like fresh salad with our carnitas. Let's go Natalia, we are going to be late. Sara, tomorrow we need you to have breakfast ready earlier. We can't be late."

"I served Tío Enrique his breakfast at 5:30. It was ready early. What time do you want breakfast tomorrow?"

"Six is good. But José is never ready at six. Okay, let's go."

José continued to eat and also almost hummed while eating, he was more like his father than mother. He also enjoys my food. Now, I just need to convince Karina I can cook up to her standards.

"Great food Sara. I hope you stay forever if you are going to cook like that," José says.

"I'm leaving next week José. I don't want to but your father says I have to go to Fish Camp. What do you know about Fish Camp?"

"Absolutely nothing. He's never mentioned it before. My dad has been very mysterious lately, he doesn't talk about his new job very much. Well, I have to go. Great breakfast, can't wait for dinner. Don't worry about my mother, she is just jealous. She's a terrible cook."

José wipes his mouth with a napkin and leaves.

CHAPTER 12

His dad is being mysterious? Why is Tío Enrique so mysterious with his own family? I need to ask Natalia what she knows, maybe she can tell me more. This is my second day in the house and I feel safer here when I'm alone. I don't have to worry about Karina's attitude or Tío Enrique yelling at me. I can do my work and relax a little.

I rush through my cleaning chores today because I know where everything is and know what to do. I put the frijoles to cook while I run upstairs to get the laundry. The laundry is in the washer while I go back to vacuum and make all of the beds. The bathrooms are easy to clean and I'm done with the upstairs in a half hour. I'm getting faster at this. I've never cleaned a house this big before but with all of the modern appliances and supplies I can get it done in a short time. I can only imagine what my mother would have done with all these machines.

While the frijoles are cooking on the stove, I begin with the salsa for dinner. The salsa can be finished when I get back from the store. I run to change the laundry from washer to dryer and put in another load. The vacuum hums as I push it around the living areas downstairs. It reminds me of Tío Enrique when he eats. That's so weird. I've never seen anybody do that. This house is so easy to clean compared to our house on the ranchito, there was always so much dust from the dry winds.

The first load of laundry is ready to fold. I pull out the clothes and put them on the counter. As I pull out a pair of jeans something drops to the floor. I finish organizing the clothes on the counter and turn around to pick up the papers on the floor, except it's not papers this time, it's money. I look down and see a wad of bills in a rubber band. I reach down to pick it up but don't want to touch it. I have to pick it up, I can't leave it on the floor. Why is there so much money in the laundry? What should I do with it? I pick it up and leave it on the tray, same as yesterday's contents I found. I can't stop looking at the money, but I try. The aroma of the frijoles reminds me of dinner and I go to the kitchen.

I hear someone in the garage and I wonder if it could be Natalia or José. I wait in the kitchen to see who comes in the house, but no one enters. It sounds like they are looking for something. What if I open the door and it's someone I don't know? Fear paralyzes me for a moment, but then I decide to run in to the laundry room and lock the door. I stand behind the locked door and listen. I glance at the money, what if someone is here to steal the money? What should I do?

"Sara? Where are you? Sara?" Tío Enrique yells.

"I'm in here, in the laundry room, Tío."

"What are you doing in there with the door closed?"

"I am frightened because of the noises in the garage, I didn't know what to do."

"No one is going to come here except family," he says as he turns and runs upstairs.

"Sara! Get up here right now!"

"Where are my jeans from yesterday? I left them here on the chair."

"In the laundry, I am washing them. Is there a problem?" He stomps back downstairs and looks in the laundry room. I can see him staring at the money in the tray. He stuffs it in his pocket, then sees the list and plastic baggie from yesterday. He picks them up and turns to me.

"Don't be so nosey, Sara. Don't go through my pockets. That is my work stuff, you don't need to look at any of that."

"Yes, Tío. But if I don't empty your pockets it will get ruined in the wash."

"From now on, if you find anything don't leave it here. I'll give you an envelope. Everything you find you put in the envelope and leave in the garage. Do you understand me?"

"Yes, Tío. I understand. I didn't know what to do with it."

"Now you know! Don't mention this to Karina or the kids, you understand?"

"Yes, Tío. I understand."

What can he be hiding from his family? Is this what José means when he says his father is mysterious? Now, I'm involved and I don't want to be. He doesn't know I read what was on the paper. He also doesn't know I counted the money. There's over $50,000 in a rubber band in his pocket. What can he be doing with that amount of money? If he has that much money he can pay off my coyote and I won't have to go to Fish Camp. He can help me if he wants to help, but he won't. He won't help me, he's made that clear. Maybe next time I find money I'l keep a few bills for myself. Will he ask me for it? Or will he think it's worth my silence? Two days here and I'm already involved in some secretive deal.

Mamá, what should I do? Papá, I don't want to steal, but I may not have a choice. I need to protect myself and Tía Elena. I'm not a thief I tell myself.

"Turn off the stove and I'll give you ride to Safeway. Come on, hurry up. I don't have all day. You can buy what you need and walk home."

"Okay, Tío. I'll be just a minute."

I run to the kitchen and turn off the frijoles and put the half made salsa in the fridge. I grab my backpack to make sure I have the money he gave me. Tío Enrique is already outside in his Explorer waiting. I don't know what to do. If I lock the door and I don't have a key, how will I get back in? I see he is getting impatient and decide to lock the door.

"Hurry up Sara!"

"Tío, I don't have a key to get back in. How do I get back in the house?"

"Tonta, see that combination near the front door? You don't need a key, you just need the combination. The combination is 181818. Don't forget it."

Why does he speak to me like that? I've never been called tonta by an adult before, especially my parents. They wouldn't dream of calling me stupid. Before we pull out of the driveway I look up to see the house number. 6715 in ceramic tile is near the front door. 6715, 6715 I need to remember that. What is the street name? I look around but don't see a street sign. I have a great memory, almost photographic. Under normal circumstances it wouldn't be difficult for me to keep all of this information in my head, but I'm stressed and forget things easily now.

"What is the name of the street?" I ask.

"Mt. Rainier, 6715 Mt. Rainier is the address."

He puts the car in gear and backs out of the driveway. By the way he speeds down the street I can tell he is in a hurry. We turn right, then left and right onto the highway. I need to remember 6715 Mt. Rainier. Right, left, right on to highway. The combination to the house is 181818. So much to remember. I reach in to my backpack for my notebook and pencil. I scribble 181818, 6715 Mt. Rainier and right, left, right on to highway. We drive about five blocks down and I see a large parking lot. We pull in and he drives up to the entrance and stops.

"This is it, go ahead. Don't forget to have dinner by six tonight."

"Tío, do you have a phone number? Can I call you if I get lost?"

He hesitates and I think he won't give me his number. I know this morning's find in the laundry makes him more careful with me. He motions for me to hand him my notebook and pencil.

"This is for you only, do not give this to anyone even my family. This is my work number. Don't call unless it is an emergency. If you call me at this number you better be almost dying."

"Gracias."

I get out of the car and walk toward Safeway's entrance. When inside I see some tables and chairs. I go and sit down right away. I'm too afraid to breathe, I need to rest and think. I need to look at my notes. I pull out my notebook and a paper falls out, on it is written Patty and a phone number. I need to call Patty, I need to talk to someone friendly. I look around but don't see any phones. I'll look on the way home.

On the page with my notes I draw a map. First I put a big square and write Safeway, next I draw a line and write highway. I remember right, left, right. So when I return it should be left, right, and left. I draw the map and place a square at the end of the turns and write 6715 Mt. Rainier. I sigh and look around. Never in my life have I had to draw a map to find my way home. Never did I have to beg for a phone number to feel safe. I've always been able to call my Papá if I needed help. I've always known I was safe. Not now, now it is a day to day thing and can be hour to hour or minute to minute. Right now I'm in a public place, I don't know anyone and I need to find my way back home. Home, if only I could go home.

The Safeway store is so big and there are so many people rushing around. They all know what they are looking for and where to find it. I grab a cart because that is what everyone else is doing. I start down an aisle in front of me and see cleaning products. The smells almost gag me and remind me of the restroom at the bus station in Caléxico. I keep going and in the next aisle I see paper towels, toilet paper and more cleaning supplies. Where is the food? I continue and find a bakery. The aroma of fresh-baked bread and sweets is overwhelming. I look at each pastry and donut in the glass case. They don't look anything like the pastries at the bakery where Tía Elena works.

Oh, Tía Elena. I miss you, I wish I was with you in San Felipe. But, I'm not and I have to be strong. I move along to the dairy aisle. I see a case full of cheeses and yogurts. I wonder if I should get some cream for the carnitas. I think I have enough money, I see something that says sour cream. Do I buy that? Maybe there is something that is just cream. I see a Mexican-looking woman in front of the dairy case. Should I ask her?

"Hola, señora. Habla español? Do you speak Spanish?"

"Sí, claro. Qué necesita hija?"

"Sour cream es crema? O hay otra crema?"

"Sí, sour cream se usa aquí. Sour cream is used here, but real cream is over in the other case next to the milk, that's what we used in Mexico."

"Gracias, señora."

"Adios."

I grab a sour cream and move down to the milk aisle to look for plain cream. I get one of those too. Who knows what Tío Enrique likes. Next I move to the meat area. There are so many choices. I see the same woman nearby.

"Señora, otra cosa. I don't know which meat to buy for carnitas, my aunt told me to not buy cheap meat."

"Ven, te enseño. Here is the meat for carnitas, Pork loin."

"Gracias."

"Hay algo más?"

"No, gracias. I am okay."

I am relieved to find people who are friendly. It is so helpful when I can ask questions in Spanish. I need only a few more things and I can start walking home. I pick up two cans of Coca Cola, some rice and cilantro. I remember to buy more tomatoes for the salsa. I walk up to the cash register and watch how others are paying for their items. Most are using credit cards, but I have cash. I see someone pay with cash and I'm relieved. I place my items on the conveyor and hope I have enough money because I have no idea how much a dollar is worth.

The young woman at the register is friendly. She asks me so many questions. Paper or plastic, how is my day, do I have plans for the day? So many questions, I just want to pay for my food.

"That's ok, no problem," she says when I don't answer all of her questions.

"Twenty-five dollars and thirty-nine cents."

I hand her fifty dollars and hope it's enough. I watch as she hands back a twenty dollar bill. She smiles and then gives me back more change and a receipt.

"Have a great day, " the young lady says.

"Thank you," I answer.

She hands me my bag of food and I walk back to the table and chairs to sit down. The woman who helped me find everything stops by and says, "Estás bien hija? Te veo uno poco triste."

"Sí, estoy bien. It's only my second day here and I'm a little confused about everything."

"Only two days? Do you need help?" she asks.

"No, estoy bien gracias," I say as I stand up and pick up my groceries.

We walk to the parking lot together and she continues to chat with me. She offers to give me a ride but I need to find my way home on my own. I look around and see a black SUV parked near her car. I look and see a man and a woman with dark sunglasses seated in the car. I have to look twice, but the woman looks very much like my friend Patty. It can't be, she must be almost in labor in LA, she can't be here. The woman looks down and reaches for something from the back seat, the man seated next to her looks away too. Does he look like Patty's boyfriend? They can't be here, but they look so much like them. Maybe I am tired and everyone looks alike to me. I finish my conversation and say good-bye.

Ok, I need to think left, right, left. No, first walk down the highway then left, right, left. Breathe, Sara breathe I tell myself. The groceries are a little heavy and I stop to put the pork loin in my back pack. Almost everything fits in my backpack except the Coca Cola. I shift the back pack up and pull the straps tight. Now, I can walk home. I must remember to buy small amounts of groceries when I come to Safeway.

As I lift my backpack up someone knocks me to the ground. I look up to see a young man running away. I hear someone yelling for him to stop, but he keeps running without looking back. Before I can catch my breath I hear footsteps running towards me. Two men offer to help me.

"Are you okay? What happened?" The first man asks.

"I don't know. Someone pushed me down."

"Are you okay? Do I need to call someone?" The other man asks.

"No, I'm okay. I just need help getting up. Who pushed me?"

"I was in my car waiting for my wife. I didn't see who knocked you down."

"I saw a young man run up and push you, then he ran away. Do you know him?" The other man asked.

"No, I just moved here. I don't know anyone," I answer.

"Let's get you back to the store so you can sit down."

"No, I'm okay. Really, I'm okay."

"Can I give you a ride?" One of the men asks.

"No, thanks. It's not far."

I grab my backpack and walk to the highway. I turn in the direction of Tío Enrique's house. I start to think I am going in the wrong direction but then notice a Burger King we passed. I continue the five blocks and turn left. My heart is beating fast but I feel a little relief when I make the final turn and see Mt. Rainier Avenue. At least I'm on the right street, it can't be far now. A few minutes later I'm at the front door and I punch in the code. The door opens and I'm inside. A wave of relief rushes through my body. Why in the world would someone push me down? Why do I feel so scared all of the time? Each day should be getting easier but it just seems to get harder and harder.

I can't control my tears, I slide down to the floor with my backpack on my shoulder and lean against the front door. This is too hard.

Mamá, Papá I miss you so much. Why is it so hard? Never in a million years did I expect to be alone like this, in the States, without my family and with an aunt and uncle who despise me. José and Natalia are nice, but if their parents tell them to not speak to me they will ignore me. They don't want to upset their parents. I look down at my pant leg and see blood on my knee. I push on the spot and it's sore but it's okay. Maybe if I get hurt I won't be able to go to Fish Camp. I don't know what is worse though, being in a place where I'm not wanted or being in a place I don't want to be. Enough Sara, get on your feet and start moving one step at a time forward. Make your way to the kitchen and get the rest of dinner started, I need to keep talking myself through these difficult situations.

My knee is throbbing by the time I finish marinating the pork loin in the Coca Cola with spices and lime. The salad, salsa and rice are finished and in the fridge. It will take over two hours to cook the carnitas so I put them in a pot to sear. Each side needs to be browned in oil, then I can pour the rest of the ingredients over the meat. When all sides are browned and the rest of the ingredients are added, I put the olla in the oven for two hours. While I wait, I go to sit in the family room and flick on the TV. Maybe I have time to relax a little while I wait for everyone to get home.

"Sara, Sara what are you doing? Are you sleeping? Did you make dinner?" Karina asks.

"Yes, it is almost ready. I sat down to watch some TV, I fell asleep. My leg is hurting."

"What? How did that happen?"

"Someone pushed me down in the parking lot at Safeway. I don't know why. I didn't notice it was bleeding until I got home with the groceries."

"Nonsense, who would push you down? Did you fall? Are you always clumsy like that?"

"No, Karina. Really, someone pushed me and two men helped me up."

"Two men, what two men?" She asks as a worried look crosses her face.

"One man was walking by and another was sitting in his car waiting for his wife. They said they saw a young man push me, but he ran away too quickly for them to see who it was. A woman from the store also helped me. They offered me a ride home but I said I would walk."

"Good, don't bring anyone to our house. Do you understand? If we don't know them we don't want them here. We are very private people. Be more careful next time and watch around you when you are walking. It was probably some young boy playing around. How much longer until dinner is ready?"

"The carnitas are in the oven, they should be ready by the time everyone arrives. The table is set and the salad is made. Go rest. It will be ready at six."

I watch her as she climbs the stairs to her room. Does she look worried? Is she concerned someone tried to hurt me? Is it possible? Maybe I need to stay close to the house until I leave for Fish Camp. I feel safer here anyway. I don't need to go shopping every day. At least I hope I don't. I still have money left from what Tío Enrique gave me, if he doesn't ask for it I'll keep it for emergencies. That's not stealing if he doesn't ask for it back. Natalia and Tío Enrique come through the door and they are arguing.

"No, Papá he's not like that," Says Natalia slamming the door.

"I saw him, I saw him grab you. He shouldn't be touching you. Do you understand me? Who is this boy anyway? Do we know his family? I don't want you near him."

"Papá, he's a friend. It's your imagination. He didn't touch me. Well, maybe he put his arm around me. But, friends do that. We are a close group of friends. You know almost everyone, you just haven't met Gary yet."

"Gary? What kind of name is that? Gary. I don't like him."

"You don't know him."

"What about Fernando or Miguel? You like them right? We know their parents."

"I don't want to talk about it. Okay? Just drop it."

"If I see you two together again we'll pick up this conversation where we left it. Now, go get ready for dinner."

I listen to their conversation from the kitchen and see Natalia run upstairs. I hope we can talk later. She is so busy with school and her friends. Karina comes downstairs in a new outfit and a smile on her face. She gives Tío Enrique a kiss and then asks him to talk in the family room.

I try to hear what they are saying, but it's difficult. If I leave the kitchen they will hear me. I turn off the stove so I can hear better. All I hear is the word mentirosa. Is Karina calling me a liar? Why would she do that? It's obvious I did fall down and hurt my knee. Why would I make up a story about a man pushing me? She must be so insecure or is there a reason I should be afraid? Maybe she is telling him because there is more danger here than I think.

José comes through the door and throws his sports bag on the floor. He says hello to me and runs upstairs. Tío Enrique and Karina come into the dining room.

"Sara, come here a minute," Tío Enrique barks.

"Sí, Tío."

"Are you making up stories? Why did you tell Karina someone pushed you down in the parking lot? Don't you think we have enough problems without you inventing more?"

"I'm not lying! Someone did push me down. Why would I lie?"

"Okay, so tell me your story and make it quick."

"Just like I told Karina, I bought the groceries and I was leaving the parking lot. I had my backpack on and carrying one other bag. Then someone pushed me and I was on the ground. When I looked up there was a man already there to help me up. Then another man got out of his car and came over and helped. I'm not lying Tío."

"Did you see who pushed you? What did he look like?"

"No, I only saw him running away. The two men said it was a young man who was running. It happened so fast they couldn't see him either."

"Okay, let's forget about it for now. Don't talk about this with Natalia or José. Let's get started with dinner."

Tío Enrique sat down and yelled, "¡A cenar, venga!" Natalia and José both came down the stairs and sat at the table. They looked worried but didn't ask any questions.

Maybe when he yells in Spanish they know not to ask questions. It's the first time I hear him raise his voice to them in Spanish.

"Sara, bring the food please. I hope you brought crema for the carnitas," says Tío Enrique.

"Yes, I did. But I had to ask someone in the store. Do you want cream or sour cream?"

José answered, "Sour cream for me please."

Tío Enrique said, "Bring both. I prefer cream, it's the Mexican style."

Good thing I brought both. I may be learning how to navigate the household and meet their expectations. As I pour crema into a container and sour cream in another I realize how in one generation tastes, dialects and food preferences can change. José prefers the American style while his dad still prefers the old recipes from Mexico.

As I set the platters on the table I watch Karina's face for approval. She doesn't show a negative or positive look. She waits to see what her family says. I sit down after serving the food and wait to hear if they like the food.

Right away I hear Tío Enrique begin to hum while he eats, a few seconds later José begins to make the same noises. I look over at Natalia and smile. Karina also smiles. I think she can't help but laugh at her husband and son for making noises while they eat. Natalia spoons some food on to her plate and passes the platter to me. I take a small portion. With all of the excitement today I'm not very hungry. I'm happy they enjoy the food but the stress of buying it, preparing it and serving it kills my hunger.

CHAPTER 13

In the next few days Natalia spends a lot of time on the phone with Gary. Whenever I go in our room she's giggling and starts whispering so I can't hear. Gary is the boyfriend her dad doesn't want her to date, a white guy. I guess he wants her to only date Hispanics or Mexicans. He thinks he can control her if he knows the parents. Natalia told me the boys he wants her to date are bad news, they aren't as nice as her father thinks.

I wonder what it would be like to only worry about boys my father doesn't like. I don't have that luxury any more. My father will never know the boys I date or the man I'll marry someday. Papá, I miss you. Mamá, I can't live without you. I never expected my life to be like this.

Each day José continues to tell me he loves my cooking. Tío Enrique doesn't say anything, but hums while he eats and I doubt he knows it, but this tells me he enjoys my food. Every day I wait for him to mention the money I found again or remind me to keep quiet about it. He doesn't bring it up until one Friday morning. Everyone eats breakfast as usual and they leave for work and school. I begin my chores of cleaning and cooking. I am very efficient with the cleaning and laundry. The cooking is a bit more challenging because I run out of ideas.

That morning Tío Enrique left at seven but returned at eight thirty with a different vehicle. I look out the window and see a large passenger van. He pulls the van into the garage and I hear him slamming doors and moving things around. A few minutes later he comes in to the house.

"Sara, where are you?"

"I'm right here Tío, in the kitchen."

"Come here. I need your help in the garage."

"Okay," I follow him to the garage.

"I need to remove these seats. I need you to lift as I release the seat from below. Can you do that?"

"Sure, I can try."

I jump in to the van and move to the first seat in the rear. He releases the seat and I lift it out of the clamp holding it in place. He pulls the seat out and places it on the other side of the garage. As I move to the other seat I see a paper on the floor. I pick it up and stuff it in my pocket. I am careful he doesn't see me, if it's nothing interesting I'll drop it when he turns around again.

He reaches in to release the next clamp and I lift the seat. We do the same on the other side. He pulls the seat out and drags it across the garage and stacks it on top of the other one. I look at the note while he is busy dragging the seat. It is in scratchy handwriting and in Spanish.

The note says, 'Ayúdame, por favor'. I wonder who needs help.

I hear Tío Enrique walk back to the van. I don't look him in the eye and I move to the last seat. He moves to the side door to release the clamp, I lift and he asks me to release the other clamp because he can't reach it. I bend over to release the clamp and I see a picture of a young girl on the floor. I move my foot over the picture and release the seat. Tío Enrique grabs the last seat and once again drags it over to the side of the garage.

"Whose van is this? Is this yours?" I ask.

"What did I tell you about being nosey, Sara? It is none of your business. It's for work. Now go back in the house and finish your chores. I need to go back to work."

As the van backs out of the garage and the door closes I wonder if there are more clues to the note in the van. Who would write a note asking for help and why did my uncle have that person in his van? I wait for my uncle to drive away and I go to where the seats are stacked. I look between the seats to see if there are any more notes. In the first seat I don't see anything, nor in the second one either. But in the third seat I find a red hair ribbon. When I pick it up I see it has some tangled black hair attached. Now, I am getting scared. First the note, then the picture and now the hair ribbon. Is my uncle transporting people in his van? Is he a coyote? How would a coyote work in Oregon? The border is in California and Arizona. Maybe there is another job he does that would explain all of this. I need to ask José again what he knows about his father's work. I stuff the picture, note and hair ribbon in my pocket and go back in the house.

Dinner needs to be prepared and I need to go to Safeway again. Tío Enrique asked me to make fajitas for dinner. I run upstairs to grab my backpack and money, he gave me even more money today to buy groceries. I keep some money in my pocket in case someone tries to rob me. I put the other half in the pocket of my backpack.

I haven't found any new items in the laundry since Tío Enrique spoke to me about the envelope. I hope I find more money in the laundry because I plan to keep a few bills each time he forgets his money in his pocket.

I walk to Safeway and I am surprised how happy I feel. I know the way to get there and it is a beautiful day. I walk past Burger King and as I get closer to Safeway I look across the highway. There is a white van like my Tío Enrique's stopped with a police car behind it. The flashing red lights grab my attention. They have a Hispanic-looking man up against the van with his hands above his head. He has his legs spread wide apart and they are searching him. I look to see if it is my Tío Enrique, but it is a heavier man. Could it be the same van? I walk away and try not to stare, but wonder what Tío Enrique is involved in. Just before I enter the store I see the police walk the man back to their car and put him in the back seat. Why are they arresting him? Is it because he isn't documented? Should I be careful? Will they stop me? Another thing to worry about.

I hurry to buy the items I need and leave the store. I don't take time to wander the aisles to look at items I could buy. I get what I need and leave. As I walk out to the highway I see a tow truck has now come to take the van away. Where will they take it? Again I worry if Tío Enrique is involved.

I walk home and am very careful. I watch in front of me, to the side and behind me the whole way home. I don't want to be stopped by the police, or pushed down by a stranger. There are too many things that could happen, all bad ones.

That evening after dinner I ask Tío Enrique if I can talk to him. He tells me to meet him in the garage after I've finished cleaning the kitchen. If he is meeting me in the garage it means something is going on, there is some secret stuff. I need to know more before I leave for Fish Camp. What if Tío Enrique is sending me some place dangerous?

"What do you want?" Tío Enrique snaps as I enter the garage.

"I saw something today that scared me."

"Like what, what did you see?"

"I saw a van on the highway just like the one you had this morning. The police were searching the man driving the van, then they towed it away. It was just like the one you brought here."

"You and your imagination, there are a lot of white vans. How could it be the same van? I'm here right? Nothing happened. Stop making up stories. You and your imagination are going to get us both in trouble. Now stop asking questions."

"Tío, is Fish Camp dangerous? Are you sending me to someplace where I could get hurt?"

"No, it's a job, nothing more. Stop asking so many questions."

He leaves me standing in the garage without a good bye, good night or go to hell. I feel so insignificant, like if I disappear he'd be happy. Papá, how could you two be related, you are so different? I understand why you didn't talk about him very much, he is nothing like you.

When I enter our room Natalia is once again on the phone with her boyfriend. I get undressed and get into bed. Natalia doesn't even have time to talk to me. She's nice to me, but I'm in the way for her too. Tears fall on my pillow and I try not to listen to their conversation. How lucky she is to have a loving family, friends and a boyfriend.

The next morning after breakfast José waits until everyone else leaves. He takes his time with his breakfast and I get impatient because it will take longer for me to clean up. But he starts a conversation and I realize he is trying to get me alone.

"Your food is delicious Sara."

"Thanks, José, I like to cook."

"When do you leave for your job?"

"I think I leave on Monday, but your father hasn't said much more about it."

"You need to make sure he get's you that job. Don't let them keep you here working as our maid. I heard my parents talking and my mother wants you to stay. My father wants you to leave as soon as possible. Make sure you leave."

"Why? You don't want me to stay?"

"No, that's not it, I want you to stay as long as you want, but my dad is mixed up in something and it's probably better if you aren't here. It has to do with his new job. Like I said, he is acting very mysterious."

"Last night I told him I saw his van stopped by the police and he got angry with me. He said there are a lot of white vans. They took the driver away and then towed the van."

"What white van? My father doesn't have a white van."

"Yes, he does. He brought it here yesterday and I helped him remove the seats. The seats are in the garage."

José's mouth falls open and he says, "I knew it, he's involved in something illegal. We never could afford a house like this before. We never had extra money. Now we can do whatever we want and he never complains about money. I wonder what he is transporting."

I don't dare tell José about the fifty-thousand dollars I found or the girl's picture and note from the van.

"Sara, don't tell my father we had this conversation. You need to be very careful and you need to go work at Fish Camp. Believe me, if he Is doing something illegal you don't want to be here. If they arrest him they'll come to the house and ask for our papers. You don't have documents and ICE will take you away and deport you."

"Maybe I want to go back to San Felipe."

"No, they won't send you back to San Felipe. They will drop you at the border in a place where you don't know anyone. A place where the narcos will be waiting. They pick you up and make you work for them. It's not a good solution for anyone. People are being dropped at the border every day. Before they can call a relative or friend to pick them up the narcos step in and take you to their compound. Then it is difficult for anyone to help you. You end up working for them forever. I have friends who have family members who disappear once they cross back in to Mexico. They never hear from them again."

"Is that true? Why do they deport people and leave them for the narcos?"

"They don't care, Sara. They just want to deport people and get them out the States. They think once they leave you in Mexico you are not their problem anymore. You need to be so careful Sara. Please make sure you go to Fish Camp. It will be a chance for you to get away from here."

"What about you and Natalia?"

"We'll be fine, we were born here. My mother has papers so she's not a problem. But if my dad is mixed up in something illegal they'll take our house and cars, they'll take everything.

"That is so sad."

"Yes, not only sad, but dangerous. I have to go to school now. You need to be careful when you go to Safeway or if you leave the house. They can pick you up anytime and ask for your ID. If you don't have to leave the house I would stay here."

"Can you help me get groceries? I need to go out today. Now I'm terrified."

"I can drive you there, but then I have to get to class. Can you walk home?"

"Yes, I'll be very quick."

José drops me in front of Safeway and waves good bye, "Be careful. See you tonight."

At least José seems concerned about my safety, but he still left me to walk home alone. It takes me ten minutes to grab the groceries I need. I pay and pack everything into my back pack. When I look up I see the man who helped me up when I was pushed the other day. When he sees me looking at him he walks in the opposite direction. A coincidence he is here at the same time? If I see the other man who helped me I'll know it's not a coincidence. The exit is a few feet away but I turn and walk to the other exit, I need to go in a different direction.

I stop to get my bearings in front of the store. What if I walk in a different direction today? What if instead of going down the highway I cut across the parking lot behind the store? There must be a street that leads to Mt. Rainier. If I get lost I can always come back and go home the way I know.

The street behind Safeway is not as wide as our street and some of the houses look almost abandoned, old cars parked on the street and garbage bins tipped over in the driveways. If I keep going straight this street should come to another street that meets up with Mt. Rainier. I remember I need to go five blocks down on the highway, if I can count five blocks on this street it should bring me out to where I need to turn. Three blocks down the street ends and I have to turn right. I need to turn left but I follow the next street. If I keep track I should be able to find my way back. But the next street curves back to the highway. I've walked quite a few blocks to end up back on the highway. At least if someone is following me they won't see me. I walk past Burger King and see a black SUV parked near the entrance. The windows are tinted and I can't see who is inside. As a kid I used to watch American TV and black SUVs with tinted windows were always the FBI, CIA or kidnappers. I'm not sure which is the safest, I start to walk faster until I can no longer see the car. When I turn the corner I look back, I see the black SUV has disappeared. At least they aren't following me. I hurry down the street and make the turn to Mt. Rainier Ave. When the house is in view I feel a little safer, but not much. The conversation with José this morning has left me terrified.

CHAPTER 14

The daily routine of cleaning and cooking helps keep me distracted. If I don't leave the house my days pass by without problems. It's when I leave the house I am terrified. José hasn't talked to me any more about his suspicions, but every night at dinner he gives me looks like he would like to continue our conversation. I wish we could talk more. Maybe we could sit and watch a movie, or I could ask him to help me with my English. After clearing the table from dinner I wait to see if José stays downstairs or retreats to his room. Tío Enrique and Karina go into their office to discuss paperwork and bills. The door to the office has never been unlocked so I haven't cleaned there. What is it they don't want me to see?

José motions for me to follow him to the family room.

"Sara, let's watch a movie."

"You read my mind. I want to watch a movie too."

He closes the double doors to the family room and puts a movie on. We both sit on the sofa so we can talk without raising our voices. He puts a finger to his mouth letting me know we need to whisper. I agree.

"Anything new happen today?" He asks.

"Yes, when I returned from Safeway I tried to take a new street but I got lost. I ended up back on the highway. When I passed by Burger King there was a black SUV in the parking lot. The kind with the windows darkened so you can't see inside."

"Did they follow you?"

"No, when I turned the corner and looked back they were gone. I don't think they followed me, at least I didn't see them."

"ICE usually has their vehicles marked. You know when they are around. Plus in this community word moves fast when they are doing sweeps. The FBI has the unmarked black SUVS and cars. They don't say FBI on the car, but everyone knows the government vehicles. Maybe the FBI is working on finding the human traffickers here in Woodburn. I've heard there is a pipeline that runs up Interstate 5 from Mexico to the Canadian border. They run drugs and people."

"What are human traffickers? It's sounds scary."

"Yes, it's the unaccompanied young girls, women and children they pick up in bus stations, train stations and along the border. Even young boys are picked up. They promise them food and a warm place to stay, they get them in a van and move them to another area where they don't know anyone. They drug them and sell them for the sex trade. It's horrible."

I think back to the two men who tried to pull me out of the bus station in Caléxico. It could have been me. Was that what they were trying to do with me? Papá, I'm terrified. I start to cry and José looks over.

"What is it?"

"That happened to me. in the bus station in Caléxico two men tried to drag me through an exit to the street. I started screaming and they let me go. A woman helped me that was riding on the same bus, so we sat together. It could have happened to me José. They tried to kidnap me."

"Sara, it is very dangerous for girls traveling alone. You have to be careful. I heard that Fish Camp isn't a great place to work, but at least you won't have to worry about ICE. You will be isolated while you are there. You need to make sure my father helps you go to Fish Camp."

"Okay, I will. I want to stay here, but I see it is dangerous here. I want to be safe and not worry about ICE or kidnappers. People talk about the States as the solution to all of their problems; a better life, more money and freedom to do what you want. But that's not true for me."

"It used to be better. Right now it is very dangerous. I hope my father isn't too involved in anything illegal. I'm going to talk to him after you leave for Fish Camp. Maybe he will tell me.

Karina and Tío Enrique open the door and walk in to the family room. Karina's face shows her dislike of the idea of her son watching a movie with me. Tío Enrique asks me to move to another chair. Karina sits next to her son and Tío Enrique sits in the recliner.

"What movie are you watching?"

I don't even know the name of the movie but José says, "Terminator."

"Do you like it Sara? Do you like Schwarzenegger?"

"Yes, I saw this movie in Mexico. I don't understand all of the English because they talk so fast, but I like it. But I'm tired. I think I'll go to bed. Good night."

I leave the room. José says good night but neither Karina nor Tío Enrique say a word. Outside the door I stop and listen.

I hear Karina say, "You be careful with her José. We don't know her. Don't get close to her and you watch to make sure she doesn't get too friendly with you. You are a handsome young man, don't let her get any ideas."

"Mamá! She's my cousin. Don't say things like that about Sara."

"Just be careful."

I hear José stand and shout, "You are the ones who need to be careful."

"What does that mean?" Tío Enrique barks.

"ICE is watching everyone. They've picked up a couple of kids from my high school. Every time Sara leaves the house she could get picked up. You know what happens to the people who they pick up, right? They drop them at the border for the narcos to grab. She would become one of their sex slaves. Do you want that to happen to her?"

"Of course not. She'll go to Fish Camp on Monday and we won't have to worry. Karina, can you get the groceries we need until then? Maybe it's not a good idea she leaves the house. We don't want any unnecessary attention brought to this house. Sara will stay here until she leaves. Does that help, hijo?"

"Yes, I think that's a good idea. Good night."

When José comes out of the family room he says to me, "It's been decided. My mom is going to do the grocery shopping until you leave. I told my dad that ICE is picking up people in town. He doesn't want anyone coming around our house so he suggested you stay in the house until you leave."

"Gracias, José. I feel safer here at home. You are a great cousin."

"Just so you know, my mom doesn't want us to get friendly. If you need to talk to me let me know. We can talk when they aren't around or are busy with other things. I won't ignore you but when they are around I won't say much to you. Okay?"

"Okay. Thanks for telling me. When we talk I feel safer because you tell me the truth."

"Good night." José says and he goes upstairs.

CHAPTER 15

Karina left the house Saturday morning to go to Safeway. She didn't ask if we needed anything, but since I'm leaving early Monday morning she will be doing the cooking again. My departure doesn't seem to make her happy. She enjoys a clean house and dinner prepared and served. It's the first time in her life someone cleans up after her. Her job at the hospital requires her to clean up after sick patients all day long. José says she always wanted someone to do the dirty work and she hoped Tío Enrique's new job would allow her to work fewer hours or even to quit her job and stay home. José says Tío Enrique still doesn't share how much he earns or how much their mortgage payments are. He tells her to be happy they can live in such a nice house and give their kids a better life.

The next morning Natalia spends most of the morning in her bedroom while I clean the kitchen. I don't need to vacuum today, just cook breakfast and lunch. Before Tío Enrique left this morning he said he is taking the family out to dinner tonight at the taqueria downtown. José tells me Luis's Taqueria is famous, even President Obama ate there when he passed through town.

I wonder if I am included in family. Will Tío Enrique take me to dinner with them or will he tell me to stay home and clean? It would be nice to go out to dinner with them, but I'm still afraid of ICE and the kidnappers. If I am with family will they approach me and ask for my papers? I don't know who to trust. I continue shining the stove and leaving the whole kitchen clean. The refrigerator is clean and ready for the new groceries Karina will bring home. José is at a soccer game and won't be back until five. He is the only one who is trying to help me. Natalia has decided she doesn't want to bother her father by being friendly to me. He won't bother her about her boyfriend if she keeps him happy. I leave the kitchen and wander back upstairs. I see José's bed is unmade and I enter to make up his room. After finishing his room I go to Tío Enrique and Karina's room. I make their bed and pick up laundry. It sure would be nice if they at least picked up their own laundry. They have become accustomed to me picking up after them. Dishes, laundry, and food, that's my job.

As I grab the laundry and head downstairs I notice another wad of money in Tío Enrique's pocket. I hold the laundry close to my chest so it doesn't fall out. On the way to the laundry room I grab the envelope he left me in the garage. The laundry is in the machine and I am once again holding $50,000. Where in the world is he getting so much money? Will he miss a few hundred if I take it? I may need money to get out of a dangerous situation. I don't think he will help me if I need it. From the roll of hundred dollar bills I take three bills, I replace the rubber band and it snaps tight around the wad of money and then put it in the envelope in the garage. I hear the automatic garage door begin to open and I know Tío Enrique is back home so I return to the kitchen. His footsteps sound all the way up the stairs and a door slams.

I hurry up to my room and close the door. Natalia is getting dressed to go meet Gary. She knows her father won't let her go out with him so she asks me to lie to her dad. She wants me to tell him she is at the library studying with a friend. I know they are going to the movies at the mall in Salem. She'll be gone most of the afternoon. If she doesn't get back in time for dinner she wants me to say she is going to eat dinner with her friend. I don't think her father is going to be very happy, he is organizing a family dinner and she might not show up. Natalia has everything she needs; a family who loves her, a boyfriend and the freedom to go out with friends. Why is she abusing this freedom? I wish I could just have my family back. I wish I could be back on the ranchito with them right now.

"Sara! Come down here."

"Okay, just a minute."

"Again you are nosey! Again you looked in my pockets. Where is it?" He asks.

"I'm doing your laundry. I put it in the envelope in the garage like you asked me to."

By the look on his face I'm not sure if he is more exasperated at me or at himself for forgetting to take the money out of his pocket. I hear him in the garage, he grabs the envelope and leaves. He must be doing something illegal to have that much money. Over the few days I've lived here he has had $100,000 in cash in his pockets. No one has that amount of cash even if they have a great job. I think José is right, it's more than mysterious, it's obvious he is doing something nasty. I wonder how long I have until he returns or Karina brings the groceries.

I want some time to myself. I open the garage door that leads to the back yard. There is a chaisse lounge. I sit down and put my feet up. On the table next to me is a newspaper. Written English is good practice for me, I pick up the paper and on the front page is a picture of a young girl. Under the picture written in large letters, HELP FIND ANGELA. I drop the paper and lean back. Do I want to read anymore? Do I want to look closer? The little girl looks like the picture I found in Tío Enrique's van. He can't be involved, he can't be that evil. I pick up the paper and start to read the article.

A local woman and her young daughter are missing. The woman's husband called police last night when his wife and young child did not return from a shopping trip. Witnesses report both were seen at the local Safeway store. Police officials say a white passenger van is thought to be involved. The missing woman's car was found parked in the Safeway parking lot. If anyone has any information about their whereabouts please contact local police. A person of interest has been taken in to custody near the scene.

I can't breathe, I look at the newspaper and I'm sure it is the same little girl in the picture I found in Tío Enrique's van. What do I do? I can't go to the police, if I go to the police they will call ICE and I'll be deported. Do I ask José what I should do? Do I dare ask Tío Enrique? If I ask him I might disappear. If it was his van used for the kidnapping they will have my fingerprints as well. He can say I was involved. I imagine if I go to the police and tell them what I know my picture can end up on the front page next. That could be me!

I sink down in the chaisse lounge and close my eyes. Papá, how did I end up here? How am I in such a dangerous situation? You always told me if I got in trouble to call you. I'm calling you but you can't help me. Mamá, Papá how could you leave me like this? None of this is my fault, I don't know what to do. Please help me. Someone please help me.

CHAPTER 16

"Where is she?" I hear Tío Enrique arguing with Karina in the family room.

"She knows we plan to eat dinner together, she knows we said we would leave at 5:30. Where is she? She better not be with that gabacho. Did she leave with him?"

"Sara, come down here right now," He yells.

"Okay, voy Tío. Voy."

"Where is Natalia? Do you know?"

"She said she was going to have dinner at her friend's house," I say.

"Which friend? Who? She didn't ask permission, Karina where is your daughter?

"She didn't say anything to me about staying with a friend."

"Sara, you better not be lying for her. Is she with her so-called gabacho boyfriend," he stares at me with hateful eyes.

"I'm not lying, Tío."

I hate she asked me to lie for her, I hate that she has a father who cares for her. I hate he is yelling at me. Most of all I hate he may have kidnapped a young mother and her child. I hate him.

He walks away and slams the door. Before I can even catch my breath he returns and yells, "Make us some dinner. We are not leaving the house until she's here. Karina, call her cell phone now. Call her friends. What is that boy's name again? Do we know his parents? Get me his number right now!"

Do I tell him I know his last name? Do I mention to José what I know?

José arrives home in the middle of the shouting match. His father questions him and asks for names. José gives his father some phone numbers to call, he also texts his sister to tell her to get home right away. It is a bit ironic Natalia is Tío Enrique's daughter and he is concerned about her whereabouts, but is he concerned about the missing little girl's father? He must be crazy with worry.

At least Natalia will come home. I don't think that little girl is coming home.

The dinner preparation takes a few minutes and I hear him pacing and yelling in to the phone, "Natalia hija, get home now. I'm very worried. Where are you?"

José calls her friends and no one will say where she is. He knows she is probably with Gary and will come home late, but he needs to feign his worry to calm his father. He leaves multiple messages on voicemail. He also continues to text his sister.

Dinner is quiet and no one says anything. I don't hear the happy sounds coming from Tío Enrique's mouth as he eats. He isn't enjoying his dinner tonight. Karina says nothing. She knows her daughter is safe, but probably with her boyfriend. It's the first time Natalia has done this but probably not the last. Tío Enrique will have to learn to deal with his teenage daughter, if he continues to try to control her she will probably do whatever she wants. If he gives her permission to date Gary she will be more compliant.

Karina's phone rings and it is Natalia. She is on her way home. She was at a movie and didn't hear the messages, she is safe and on her way. Tío Enrique pushes his plate away and leaves the table. The door to his office slams and we hear him screaming and swearing. José and Karina ignore the sounds coming from the office. I know this isn't over, when Natalia comes home there will be more screaming and arguing.

At this moment I hate Natalia, she has everything and she is causing all of us to listen to this rage. Is she selfish? Is she unaware of what she has? I'd like to tell her how I feel, I'd like to tell her about the two-day bus trip, the news of my family's death, my helpless Tía Elena in San Felipe and the threat of deportation I live with every day. The fear and loneliness I live with while she is out with her novio at a movie. I hate her, I hate Tío Enrique and I hate Karina. I need to leave this house, I need to start a new life without this drama. But what can I do? I'm alone in a country that doesn't want me, in house with a family who doesn't want me either. I'm a foreign object, not a person, but an object that is in the way. I need to leave. If I run away they won't care, I need to make a plan and if that plan includes Fish Camp that is what I will do, clean fish.

The screaming wakes me from a sound sleep. At first I'm not sure where I am, but then I hear Tío Enrique's raised voice.

Natalia is screaming at him, "You said you wouldn't give me permission to date Gary, so I went anyway. Sara is the same age and she gets to do whatever she wants, you are letting her go away for six weeks to work. You won't let me go one day on my own without telling you where I am and who I'm with. You don't seem too worried about what can happen to her while she is gone."

"She is not my daughter. The end. I don't want to discuss this anymore. Go to bed."

Natalia enters the room and falls on her bed. Her sobs are hard to ignore, but I don't want to comfort her. She compared her princess life to mine. There is no comparison. I turn over and pretend to be asleep.

The next morning at breakfast Natalia doesn't join her mother, she grabs her backpack and says she is getting a ride to the library. Karina sighs and doesn't argue as Natalia leaves the house. She probably suspects that Natalia is going to see Gary but she knows that her daughter has declared war on her father's authority. I think that the quiet teenage years have ceased. They no longer have control over their daughter. Karina probably did the same thing when she dated Tío Enrique.

Today is my last day here with family. Tomorrow I leave for Fish Camp, for whatever work they give me. Fear fills my body from my toes all the way up to the tips of my hair. I don't know if I have ever been this afraid before. Each part of my trip I thought was the worst, but it gets more terrifying every day.

Tío Enrique tells Karina to buy me clothes for work. She doesn't ask me to go along, she leaves the house in a huff and is gone for a few hours. When she returns she hands me two bags of clothes in blue Walmart bags. She doesn't bother to wait for a thank you. She walks away. I'm not sure if she is mad because she had to spend money on me or because she will have to return to cooking and cleaning tomorrow. I carry the bags upstairs and lay them on the bed. In one bag is a pink sweatshirt, not my favorite color, and some jeans. I try them on and they fit, they aren't flattering but I guess it doesn't matter. It's not like I'm looking for a novio or anything. There is also a pair of tennis shoes, socks and underwear. In another bag there is another pair of jeans and a black-hooded sweatshirt and a few men's t-shirts. Basics, no shampoos, no girly items only what she thinks I should wear. It would be nice to buy a few personal items before I leave, but since I no longer leave the house alone it's almost impossible. If Natalia were friendlier I could ask her but I doubt that is going to happen. Maybe if I look around in the bathroom I can find a few items I need.

It seems like they don't even treat me like a human being. The clothes Karina bought are like a purchase she would make for an unknown person they are giving charity to, no personal touches, no favorite colors and no fashion. The clothes I've been wearing since I arrived are very tired looking, one outfit is washed and dried every day. I wear one while the other is in the laundry.

I miss the days when my mother would take me shopping. We would look for cute outfits, last summer she bought me some sundresses I loved. I wore them all summer. This summer I'm stuck wearing jeans and now men's t-shirts with a pocket. No fashion sense there. My backpack overflows with the new outfits. I need a bigger bag for my clothes even though everything I own, my total existence is here on top of the bed. Natalia's closet is bulging with clothes I never see her wear. She has so many outfits she won't notice if I borrow a few things. Her father will buy her new ones if she asks. A Levi jacket is pushed back in behind the other outfits. I've never seen her wear this or even take it out of the closet. She won't miss it. On the floor are three pairs of Nike tennis shoes. Who needs three pairs? She won't miss those either, I grab a pair and make room in my backpack. A jean jacket, a pair of tennis shoes and one more thing. I look through her summer dresses and find a fitted sun dress with small red and black polka dots. Mine now! I also see a larger backpack. I grab it because I need it.

Self pity doesn't help anyone, the new outfits help me to gain a little more self confidence. Natalia's self confidence needs no boost, she has everything she needs. Plus, no one will even notice. In the bathroom under the sink is a travel make up bag with small bottles of shampoo, conditioner, make up, toothpaste and deodorant. I glance around and see a mascara, hairbrush and comb. Since she doesn't use them everyday they will never be missed. Adios, prima mía. Thanks for your support and friendship.

CHAPTER 17

Monday morning comes too quick for me. Today is the day I leave for the next chapter of my life. What will Fish Camp bring? Papá, I am trying so hard but it is so hard without you. Mamá, I miss you so much. I can't stand the thought that I'll never see you again. You would be ashamed of me, I've stolen money and clothes. I never would have done that before, but now it doesn't even bother me. I feel entitled because of how much they have and how little I have. My borrowed backpack is on the floor and stuffed full. I don't want to ask for anything from anyone. I want to leave all this behind and move on.

Breakfast of course needs to be made. I start working in the kitchen and distract myself a little. Bacon, eggs, chilaquiles and salsa. That's all I'm making. Café con leche and good enough. They won't have me here to make their breakfast anymore.

Tío Enrique has returned to making joyful noises while he eats, he must not be worried about anything today. He could say thank you, or this is delicious, or I'm going to miss your cooking.

But no, never a kind word for me. That's okay, I don't plan on returning here if I can help it. I eat alone in the kitchen and wrap up a few tortillas, chiles and cheese for my lunch. Who knows when I'll eat again or if they will give me lunch at Fish Camp. I know nothing about it.

"Let's go Sara, we need to get to the van by 7:30. You can't miss the pick up time. Grab your stuff and meet me in the car," he says as he slams the kitchen door that leads to the garage.

I look around, no one got up to say good-bye, no one left me a note to wish me well. José didn't even talk to me last night. Natalia doesn't seem to care if I stay or go. Her initial friendliness wore off when she realized she'd lose points with her father if she was friendly to me. Of course Karina is not around, she'll wait for me to leave before coming down today. She isn't happy she is losing her maid, but she has no desire to see me off or wish me well. Well, it was nice to have a warm place to sleep, but I realize now, more than ever, I have no family to rely on here.

Tío Enrique is waiting in the driveway with the Explorer running, he looks very impatient. I know he wonders how much I've figured out and how careful he needs to be with me. I won't say anything to anyone if I can get away today and go to Fish Camp. Fear keeps me from telling anyone.

"Let's go, Sara. We're in a hurry. If you miss the pick up you won't be able to go to Fish Camp. We both know what that means, right?"

"I'm not sure what that means, does it mean I'll go later?" I ask.

"You know what it means. Karina and the kids know you are leaving, they don't expect you back at the house. Your Tía Elena has no idea where you are. No one is waiting for you. It's just you and me. He reaches over and grabs my hand."

"You're scaring me, Tío," I say as I push his hand away.

"You should be scared. You are too nosey for your own business, you have a big imagination. You know none of the things you think happened really did happen, right? But, if you continue to nose around I know plenty of men who would enjoy your company."

"I don't know anything. I didn't see anything. Don't worry Tío, you don't have to worry about me," I answer and wonder how my father's brother could even think of selling his niece to sex traffickers.

"Good, I think we will get there in time. It's a few miles down the road."

What if there is no such thing as Fish Camp, what if there isn't a job for me. Maybe he invented it to get rid of me. José knows he is up to something, but he'll never question his father if I disappear. I think about jumping out at the next red light, but where would I go? If I have no place to go ICE will find me and deport me for sure. My only possibility is to hope Fish Camp is a real job and we are headed there to meet up with the other workers. My breathing becomes difficult and I lower the window on my side. I gasp for some fresh air. We are in the countryside and the green fir trees pass by in a blur. The smell of rain and earthiness is pleasant, a smell I'm not accustomed to. The Oregon countryside is beautiful even on this rainy, misty morning. The Explorer slows and I see a gas station ahead on the right.

"Remember, you need to earn as much as possible to pay off the coyote. I'm not paying that for you. You need to try very hard to get that debt paid," he says as he turns in to the gas station.

There is a white van, not unlike my Tío Enrique's van, waiting near the side of the building. I see seven to eight people leaning up against the van waiting. I hope we aren't late and they are waiting for me, that would be a terrible way to start. A horrible thought comes to my mind, what if Fish Camp is code for sex trafficking?

The Explorer door slams and Tío Enrique walks away to talk with friends leaning against their older model cars near the front door of the convenience mart. He doesn't even say good bye, he just walks away. It's hard for me to move, if I get out of the truck I'll be on my own. If I stay in the truck and return with Tío Enrique who knows what will happen to me. My decision is to step out of the vehicle and walk over to the group waiting by the van. I hesitate and then step out of the Ford Explorer. I am reminded how the situation could be worse when I hear my uncle's voice across the parking lot. He did threaten to make me disappear or loan me out to friends.

I look over at the group of men laughing and patting each other on the back. I feel even more uncomfortable, the only thing I can do is to go over and stand near the group next to the van.

The group is mostly made up of women. There are two young men and the rest are women. All with hispanic features, some speaking Spanish others speaking English but all dressed in jeans, sneakers and hooded sweatshirts. Karina had been right in her purchase, I will fit right in.

A tall woman about my mom's age calls out to me in English. "Are you Sara? C'mon over. We're all waiting for the driver to come back, then we'll leave. Your uncle told me you need this job so let's hope you do well. Have you worked at Fish Camp before? My name is Magda," she says as she holds out her hand.

I shake her hand and answer, "No, it is my first time. I'm not sure what I need to do. I don't know anything about Fish Camp."

"Don't worry, we train you. I'll have you sit next to me in the van when we start the trip. You'll need to practice your English. I'll help you." responds Magda.

The group gathers around Magda like chicks to a mother hen, it is obvious to me that the others regard her as the person in charge. I hope she will help me with my English, but more than that I hope Magda will be a friend. I need a friend if I'm going to survive the next six weeks at Fish Camp. Madga has a serious, but pretty face and she is tall and slender. Her smile and her kindness shows through the serious exterior.

"Vicky, this is Sara. This is her first time at Fish Camp. I hope you will help her out if she has any questions." Magda nudges Victoria in my direction so she would have to say hello.

"Hi, I'm Victoria but everyone calls me Vicky," Victoria shakes hands with me and leaves me standing outside the van as she jumps into the front seat.

"Okay, everybody listen up," Magda switches from English to Spanish so everyone understands.

"There are twelve of us, and there are fourteen seats with seat belts. We don't want anyone riding without a seatbelt. That leaves some extra space for your backpack or your lunch bags. Don't put your suitcases or duffel bags up front. Give them to Jaime and he'll put them in the back or up on top. Any questions?"

The others soon jump into the seats behind Magda and I. It's obvious to me that the others are a bit crowded, but Magda doesn't invite them to share our seat.

Jaime closes the doors and jogs to the front of the van. He steps into the driver's seat and starts the van. Soon we are are on our way down highway 99 toward Salem. The trip to Fish Camp has begun and already I've relaxed a little. I check my seat belt and rearrange my lunch bag and backpack to make room for Magda to put her things.

Magda stretches her long legs out until they reach under the driver's seat. She appears to relax a little also, at the same time she looks a little worried. As we approach Salem she is already staring out the window as images of berry fields whizz by.

The two young men sitting in the back seat of the van talk about the soccer game they played the weekend before. The conversation stops and I notice they both are plugged in to headphones.

"How much time to Fish Camp?" I ask Magda.

"See, you do speak a little English. It will take us about two hours, sometimes less. It depends on the traffic and the rain. Jaime drives slower when it rains," Magda says as she turns her eyes to look out the window once again. This is my hint to not bother her, Magda stares out the window like she is in her own world. I know she doesn't want anyone else to intrude on her world.

I relax a little thinking that Magda can be a good friend. Maybe I would even learn a little English along the way to Fish Camp. I notice two other girls my age and hope they also will be friendly.

"Victoria, you could help Sara by speaking English with her.," Magda says.

"Whatever," Vicky turns around and slouches down in the seat and puts her head against the window and closes her eyes.

Magda explains to me, "Victoria came to the U.S when she was two years old, or rather her parents brought her to the U.S at that age. She is ambivalent about her status as a child of farmworkers. Her angry attitude stems from the language issue in her own home. While she loves her parents, they embarrass her when she has to translate for them or help them with bills and paperwork. She just wants her parents to fit in, something she knows will never happen. Because she has no control over what her parents do, she decided to stop speaking Spanish unless it was necessary. She speaks Spanish to them at home, but when in public will only answer them in English. This decision makes it even more difficult for her parents. When they asked her to give up her senior year to help the family by working she stopped speaking to them completely. If she is going to earn money to feed the family, she is going to do whatever she wants."

I hear the two girls behind me speaking Spanish. I could only hear parts of each sentence because the van is noisy. I hear things that worry me. I hear the one girl mention seasickness and vomiting. Why in the world would they be talking about seasickness? I wonder. Where exactly is Fish Camp?

Then I hear something that scares me to death, "...then she fell overboard and it took three guys to get her back on board. Lisbet said she would never return to Fish Camp again. She was so cold when they got her back on the ship she couldn't get warm. They wrapped her in blankets and kept feeding her soup. She said it was terrifying. She said she would rather work in the cannery than return to Fish Camp."

The next thing I hear, "Nasty old man, he needs to keep his hands to himself. The next time he tries to touch me I'm going to give him a kick and you know where," The two girls giggle but seem distressed about the man they mention.

Not only is there seasickness, but the possibility of falling overboard and now they talk about a dirty old man. Fish Camp is sounding less and less appealing the closer we get. My stomach starts to churn and I feel like I'm going to suffocate. Not now, not another anxiety attack. I start to breathe in short breaths and think about happier times.

Just then, Magda leans over and says, "Are you all right? You look a little nauseous."

"Estoy bien," I lie.

"Maybe you're hungry. We'll stop soon and eat. The fresh air and some food will settle your stomach."

"Jaime, how much longer until we arrive at the next rest stop?"

"Unos diez minutos," answers Jaime looking in the rearview mirror as he answers Magda.

"Okay, thanks Jaime."

"Everybody listen up, we'll be stopping in 10 minutes. There are some restrooms and picnic tables. It looks like the rain has stopped and we can sit at one of the tables and eat. Did everyone remember to bring a lunch? You know your meals at Fish Camp don't start until we are onboard."

The idea of eating with total strangers makes me lose my appetite. I need to start getting used to it. Sometimes the sadness overwhelms me and I want to fall down a hole and never come out. It feels like I never lived at Ranchito Gutierrez. I feel like I never spent summers with my Tía Elena in San Felipe making her salsa. Sometimes I wish I could push rewind and go back to being a six year old riding one of my dad's horses. I know that isn't possible but I wish it were. I want to close my eyes and wake up to my old life.

After a quick picnic lunch at the rest stop everyone starts toward the van. I wad up the aluminum foil I had wrapped tortillas in. I look around for a garbage can and can't see one on the way to the van so I shove the garbage back into my bag.

I notice when I get back into the van Magda and Vicky have switched seats. I'm now back to being on my own. Magda returns to her leader role and it looks like the friendly smile on her face disappears forever.

"Sara, you can sit next to Victoria and start practicing some English conversation if you want to survive on board."

I jump in to the seat next to Vicky. She ignores me and closes her eyes with earplugs hanging from her ears. It's obvious she doesn't want to be friends. The van starts up and we drive along the curvy highway. The roads in Baja can be very curvy and treacherous, but this road seems so dangerous in the rain; one hairpin curve after another. I try to close my eyes so I can't see what is ahead of us. Beads of sweat start to pop out on my forehead and things start to get blurry.

Oh no. Not now, not again. I close my eyes and try to take small breaths to relieve the beginning of another anxiety attack. Nausea takes over and I need fresh air. How much longer will I have to ride in this van, each minute my anxiety increases and I start to shake.

One of the girls puts her hand on my shoulder and I turn to see her talking to me but I can't hear anything. The panic is so intense I can't hear what she is saying. I don't even know if she is speaking Spanish or English, I can't hear a thing. The next thing I know the van has pulled over and the door next to me opens. Magda is speaking to me but I don't understand a thing.

The two boys in the back jump out of the van and talk with Magda. They help me to sit on an upside down crate someone had pulled from the back of the van. Shivers run down my spine until someone wraps me in a blanket, then they hand me hot coffee from a thermos. I try to sip the hot coffee and things start to come back into focus.

I hear Magda saying, "Sara, Sara are you okay? Sara answer me. Nod your head yes if you can hear me," Magda urges. The conversation around me starts to make sense. I can hear Magda's voice pleading with me, "Sara, please just shake your head yes if you hear me."

At that moment a logging truck passed by and a huge gust of wind rattles the doors on the van and sprays everyone with mist from the wet road. I look up at Magda and nod my head yes.

"I think she's come back to us. Does anyone know what happened? Girls did you see what happened before she left us for another planet?"

"No Magda, we were talking and she started shaking. I leaned over to tap her on the shoulder and she didn't answer me. That's when I yelled up to you that something had happened to Sara."

Just then I lean over and vomit. Magda leans over and holds my hair back from my face.

"It's ok Sara, you'll feel better now. Here are some tissues, wipe your face. Do you feel better?"

My head bobs up and down, I answer yes. But I then lean over and vomit again.

"Oh dear, we're going to be late. Let's get everyone else back in the van, I'll change seats with Sara. Maybe she gets carsick. That's not going to be pleasant when we get on board. Pobrecita," Magda looks at her watch.

"Everybody, let's get going. Sara will be okay in a minute. We'll give her some fresh air and a plastic bag. We can hope she'll make the rest of the trip." Magda directs everyone like she was the ringmaster in a circus. "¡Vámonos!"

Magda helps me stand and walks me along the edge of the curving highway watching for more log trucks. We stopped in the worst place ever, trucks can't see us until they are right on top of us. With luck any driver that comes over the hill won't slam on the brakes. Experienced drivers know better than to slam on the brakes. But you never know if some inexperienced driver will came over the hill, the driver could kill us all.

"Sara, let's go. We have to move out of this spot. It's dangerous here. Get in the front seat and see if you can make it to our drop site," Magda pushes me toward the front seat.

Still too weak to resist, the two boys somehow get me into the van and close the door. Magda jumps in the back seat and hands me a plastic Safeway bag.

"Here, if you're going to be sick, please use this.."

The girls in the back hand me some chewing gum. One of the boys in the back passes forward a cold coke for me to hold against my forehead. I smile and take the gum and the soda. The cold soda feels good as I hold it to the back of my neck and feel better. The gum also helps me tame the vile taste in my mouth and helps me rinse my mouth so I don't vomit again. I swallow the flavored mint juices from the gum and feel a tiny bit better. Magda places a folded up sweatshirt under my head and tells me to lean against the window. I sleep for the rest of the trip.

The next thing I hear is when the conversation starts to get louder and I smell the salt air. I had fallen asleep. I lift my head and wipe the drool from my mouth and look around to see if anyone notices. Much to my relief everyone is busy unloading the van and pays no attention to me.

The shining sun surprises me, I heard in the van that Fish Camp can be gloomy and rain for days. The sun streams through the van windows and I see steam rising from the wooden plank dock. The van is parked right on the dock and all around I see water. We are on a dock in a bay and everyone is unloading the van. I watch as the others walk toward the end of the dock where there is a fishing vessel moored.

Magda bangs on the door of the van and says, "Let's go Sara, we're here! No time to dilly-dally. Let's get going, grab your gear and follow the others."

I look at Magda with a worried look on my face. "I thought we are going to a Fish Camp, why is everyone getting on that fishing boat?"

Magda looks at me and laughs, "Do you mean your uncle didn't explain what Fish Camp is? He didn't tell that it is six weeks at sea on a fish-processing vessel? I wonder what else he didn't tell you."

"No, he says I'm lucky to get this job, that's all. I thought we would be camping and processing fish caught by the local fishermen. I had no idea I would be on a ship. Do I have to go?"

"Not much choice now, they contracted you and your passage is part of your pay. You need to work it off. Let's go. You'll figure it all out when we get there. Come on," Magda says without smiling.

I get out of the van and grab my backpack. I follow Magda along the slippery dock. I hope for a moment a wave will wash me off the dock and someone will have to rescue me. But if that happens I'd need to go back to live with Tío Enrique and I don't want that. I hope this is all a dream.

Papá help me. I don't want to do this. Mamá, please I need someone to take care of me, I'm tired. I need you.

"Don't even think about falling in Sara, others have tried it. We just pull them out of the water and put them on the boat all wet. Worse for them, they have to spend four hours in wet clothes."

"Four hours?"

"Yes, it takes at least four hours to catch up with the larger vessel. They are already at sea. This is just the beginning, muchacha."

At the end of the dock I see everyone else has already boarded the fishing boat. I look over at Magda to see if she'll tell me what to do, but she ignores me and jumps down on to the boat. I follow her and land on the deck of the moving boat. I already don't like this.

Four hours at sea on this tiny fishing boat. I can see the nets and fishing gear hoisted out of the water. The black smoke from the ship's engine already is making me gag. The loud banging of the engine is making it impossible to even hear what others are saying. I see everyone has stowed their gear below deck and found places to sit. It looks like some have even found places to nap in the sun. I find it hard to walk on the deck. The two boys from the back of the van watch me and laugh.

They both run over to me and say, "Watch us, you have to learn to walk on water. Watch us. Stand with your feet apart and walk like this."

The two boys walk away from me with their feet spread wide apart.

"You need to walk like this on board, and always hang on to the railings. You never know when we will get hit with a wave." The taller boy grabs my bag and takes it below.

"Here come and sit with us, we have a nice spot in the sun. It will be the most protected spot when we get out on open sea."

"What is your name?" I ask.

"Teodoro, me llamo Teodoro. Te adoro Sara."

We both laugh at the play on language he uses to introduce himself.

"Te adoro....I adore you, in English."

"Gracias por ayudarme, Teodoro. Mucho gusto," I smile.

"No problem, Sara. I know how difficult it is the first time."

"How many times have you been to fish camp?"

"I started when I was fourteen. I lied and told them I was sixteen."

"How old are you now?" I ask.

"Nineteen, I've been coming to fish camp for five years now. It get's better, the first one is the hardest," Teodoro laughs.

"The first time I was so sick and swore I would never come back, but here I am for the fifth year. It's better than the cannery, you get to see a little of the coast and be outside. My parents both worked in a cannery and they said they never wanted me to work there."

"What if I get seasick? I've never been on the ocean before, only the bay in Mexico. I'm afraid of the ocean."

"Everybody gets sick at first, but you'll get used to it."

"I've heard Norpac isn't a nice place to work. Do they still work there? Are they at Norpac," I ask.

"No, they.....aren't, They don't work anywhere anymore. They both died." Teodoro stammers.

My eyes fill with tears, "Oh, I'm so sorry. I know what that is like. My family also died a few weeks ago. I'm the only one left."

Teodoro looks at me and grabs my hand. "Sara, I hope we can be friends. I'd like to show you how Fish Camp works so you don't suffer the way I did. Will you let me help you?"

"Yes, please. I'd like a friend. I had to leave my friends behind in Baja. I don't know anyone."

Miguel returned from stowing my gear and grabs the railing.

"How are you doing Sara?" Teodoro drops my hand and looks away.

"Fine Miguel. Teodoro says he will help me learn how to survive at Fish Camp. Will you help me too?"

"At your service, Sara. We both will be here for any questions you have. Now I think you should sit down because we're about to leave the dock."

The boat bobs up and down and I'm terrified I'll get sick again. I almost wish the boat would break down or something would happen to prevent us from leaving the dock. My wish doesn't come true. I watch two men untie the big ropes tied to the dock and place them in a pile on the deck. After the ropes are in place the two men walk to the back of the boat and light a cigarette. One offers Magda a cigarette and it's obvious they are friends. How long will it take for me to make friends here?

A feeling of loneliness sweeps through me like someone stabbed me in the heart. The boat moves in reverse and turns to move through the marina. Magda, along with the two men stand at the back of the boat talking and laughing. They act like they are on a Sunday cruise. They don't seem at all worried about the four-hour trip ahead of them or the six weeks of living on a ship.

"Your language will get mixed up for a while. Don't worry about it. Speak English or Spanish. Most people here understand both. But on the ship you will need to learn some more English. Not everyone there speaks Spanish."

"What is it like? What is it like to be on the ship? Will I like it?"

"Bueno, Sara ... it won't be like anything you have ever done before, but it's not bad. You can make friends and you can have some fun, but it is hard work and long hours. Mr. G. is our supervisor, he will be assigning our jobs. The ship is huge and there are a lot of people working there. Some people work full time for the company and they make great money. Some of them start at $45,000 and can make up to $75,000."

"What? How? ¿Cómo? ¡Necesito ganar mucho dinero!"

"¡Tranquila Sara, tranquila!"

"I didn't know we could earn that much money. I can pay off my bills and I won't need to be here as long. I can go back to San Felipe and live with my Tía."

"Sorry. Lo siento. We don't make that much money. We have a contract and get paid by the week. They also deduct money to pay our transportation to the ship."

"I don't know anything about what I will be doing. I don't know how long we work or what I need to do. Teodoro, I'm so afraid I won't be able to do the work."

Unlike Magda and the others, it concerns me how the next six weeks will work out for me. I can't remember a time since my parent's death that I've felt happy or safe.

The thought of being "out-to-sea" terrifies me. I'm happy that Miguel and Teodoro invited me to sit with them. They seem to know what to expect and maybe they will help me.

The boat chugs out of the harbor, the boat's noise and exhaust cause the bile to rise in my throat. I choke it back and try not to get sick again. The rocking of the boat has a calming effect on me. I rest my head on the cushion and drift off the sleep.

The squawking of the gulls wakes me and I open my eyes. At first I forget where I am. I look around and notice Vicky is feeding seagulls pieces of bread from a Safeway bag. She stands at the back of the boat and holds her hand in the air with a piece of bread. The seagulls dive bomb her and grab the bread from her hand. As they do this they scream and nip at the bread. I sit and watch for a few minutes before I realize Teodoro is staring at me.

"Did you sleep well? ¿Dormiste bien?" asks Teodoro.

"Yes, I mean sí … no sé."

"What if I get seasick? What if I can't keep up with everyone else?"

"There are lots of different jobs on the ship. They will train you and show you what you need to do, but once you learn the job they will move you onto another job. They like to move people around so you don't get bored. Some of the jobs are better than others. They pay us usually at the end of the six weeks and it can be $1000-$1200."

"¿Nada más?"

"No, unless you work non-stop and don't sleep and you can't do that."

"What do I do? I'll never be able to pay off the coyote. Oh, I mean … pay my bills."

"Sara don't worry, everyone here came by way of a coyote at one point. Don't let it embarrass you. We all have similar stories and you will hear some of the them once you start meeting people and making friends."

"I feel so helpless. I won't make enough money to pay off the coyote. Is there any way out of this?"

"Don't worry about it ... we'll think of something. Once you start working we can talk. I have some ideas."

"¡Díme! Tell me!"

"No, not yet. You are so overwhelmed now. Let's just take one day at a time. We have about one more hour before we arrive. Do you want anything to eat? Magda brought sandwiches and cookies for us. Let's go get something to eat."

I follow Teodoro. While he opens the cooler and looks for sandwiches I glance out over the side of the boat. The water is choppy and the boat bounces up and down, but I walk on the boat as Miguel had shown me. I'm starting to feel a little more comfortable and realize I'm hungry.

Teodoro shows me two sandwiches and asks, "Tuna or Ham?"

"Can I try both? Can we share?"

"Yes, fifty-fifty, we can share. There's hot coffee downstairs. Do you want coffee?"

"Maybe after we eat."

We both realize we are very hungry, there is no need to keep the conversation going. Other people seem to not even notice us sitting together and eating our sandwiches until Miguel sees us. I see Miguel walking toward us and I give him a smile.

"¿Qué tal Sara? How is it going?"

"Mejor, gracias Miguel. I slept a little bit and I didn't realize I was hungry. Now un café con leche will make me feel even better."

"¡Fantástico Sara! Glad you are feeling better. Don't let Teodoro tell you any scary stories."

Teodoro flashes a dirty look at Miguel but doesn't say a word.

"Scary stories? What? I don't understand," I say

"¡Que no te cuente historias de miedo!" Miguel says.

"Miguel, stop. Why are you doing this? Déjala."

"Teodoro, do you have historias de miedo?" I ask.

Teodoro turns and gives Miguel a look that would leave most people cold, and walks away leaving me and Miguel standing next to the coffee machine.

"¿Qué pasó? I don't know what happened. Why did he leave?"

"Teodoro has some bad history. You don't want to hear his stories. Plus you can never believe a word he says. Es un mentiroso."

"¿Qué? Teodoro un mentiroso? A liar? Por qué?"

"I've known him for years and he has a lot of stories he tells that never happened."

I walk away with my cup of coffee and now don't know who I can trust. I like Teodoro and now Miguel has put a lot of doubt in my mind. Maybe I should just stay to myself. I go back up on deck and find a place to sit by myself. I stare out at the ocean and wonder how my life has become so complicated.

Vicky comes over and sits down next to me, "You sure are getting a lot of attention from those two."

"What two?"

"Teodoro and Miguel. They seem like they want to be your novio. Well, they seem very interested in you. Which one do you like?"

I think for a moment and wonder why Vicky is so interested. People who had been below deck napping start to come out on deck. I notice people look excited and have smiles on their faces. How could they be excited about working at Fish Camp? The fishing boat starts to slow down and I turn to look toward the front of the ship and I see a large fishing vessel. On the side of the ship are the words Sea Freeze and in huge letters PescaConga. I wonder why they use the name Pesca which means to fish in Spanish. Could it be a Mexican ship? Or a Mexican company? I notice the American Flag flying on the top of the ship. Maybe Teodoro knows, then I think, Who can believe what he says?

Both Teodoro and Miguel come over to me, "Sara, hurry we will be arriving soon. Grab your things and get ready to get on the SeaFreeze.

"Qué quiere decir "Sea Freeze?"

"It's a play on words of Sea Breeze which is Brisa del mar, they changed it to Mar congelada. It's because they freeze the fish on the ship. It is a freezer vessel.

"¿Y PescaConga? What is that?"

"Pesca de pescar and Conga de congelar. It's a company originally from South America. It's an American company now but they never changed the name. Make sure you have everything, if you forget something you won't ever see it again. How many bags do you have?"

"Just this one, I don't have too many things."

"Don't worry Sara, you won't need many things on board the Sea Freeze," Says Miguel.

"Watch how they open a huge door on the back of the ship! Our boat will pull up next to it and if the water isn't rough you can just jump over the edge and get onto the ship."

"What if the water is rough?"

Miguel and Teodoro look at each other and then Teodoro says, "You don't want to know. The water isn't too bad today. But you have to hurry and listen for instructions. The captain gets angry when it takes more than 10 minutes to move us from the smaller boat to the larger fishing vessel."

"Let's go Sara, here take my hand," says Miguel as he offers his hand to me.

I look at both Teodoro and Miguel and then take Miguel's hand. I don't care who helps me as long as I don't fall in the water.

"Ok, we're next. We're going to walk through this small door they have opened and walk right onto the ship."

"But it's moving a lot! ¡Se mueve mucho! The other ship is in the water, what if I fall?"

"Come on Sara, both of us will hold on to you. Take Teodoro's hand too. ¡Here we go, a la una, a las dos dos, a las tres, salta!"

We all jump and I don't let go of either of their hands until we are 20 feet away from the water. I am still trembling when I finally let go of their hands.

"¡Dios mío qué miedo! Oh my God I was so afraid. Thank you for your help."

Teodoro points to a man watching from the catwalk above, "That's Mr. G., our boss."

As we enter the hallway Magda is waiting for me, "So, you made it Sara! I wasn't sure if you were going to make it or not. Here come with me, you will be sharing a bunk with the women. I put you and Vicky together."

I look at Teodoro and Miguel. They both smile and say, "See you at dinner Sara. Don't worry."

I follow Magda down the long hallway. The movement of the ship gives me a dizzy feeling, but not as much as I had on the smaller fishing boat. What I do notice is the unmistakable smell of the ocean and fish. I will just have to get used to the smell because for the next 6 weeks I will be eating, sleeping and dreaming about fish.

Magda shows me the room I'll share with nine other women. The room looks like what I think an army barracks must look like. There are five bunk beds, two on each wall and one at the end of the room.

Vicky calls as I enter, "Over here. I've got the top bunk, you can have the bottom one. I hope you don't snore."

I understand Vicky enough to know she has given me the bottom bunk. I don't know what snore means. I grab the striped sheets and start to make my bed carefully folding the corners like my mom taught me. I realize I haven't thought about my family in almost four hours. It's the first time since the accident I haven't thought about them. Tears roll down my cheeks and I place the top blanket over the sheets. After putting the pillowcases on the pillows I sit on my bunk.

Everyone around is busy talking and laughing. I can't think of anything to laugh about. I wish I knew more of what to expect for the next six weeks. I unpack my clothes and place them in the two-drawer stand next to the bed. As I unpack my clothes a picture drops to the floor.

When I pick it up Vicky grabs it from me and says, "Who are these people? Is that your Mom and Dad? How come they didn't come with you?"

I grab the picture back and stuff it in my drawer. "¡Están muertos!" and I run from the room. I run into the hallway and head in the direction where I think the bathroom should be. I open the door and enter one of the stalls and sit down and start sobbing. For the first time all day I let the tears flow like I have never cried before in my life. I hear the door squeak open.

"Hey! You ok?"

I sniffle and try to stop sobbing, "No! No estoy bien."

"Hey, I speak a little Spanish but can we speak English? What happened? Are you new?" The voice asks.

"Yes, today is my first day and I hate it very much. I didn't know I was going to be on a smelly ship. Vicky took my picture."

"What happened?"

"My parents are dead, my uncle doesn't want me living with him and now I have to work here on this fish ship for six weeks."

"Is that all?" The voice laughed.

I open the stall door and look out. Standing before me is a short, dark-skinned girl with dark eyes and beautiful long black hair. She is dressed in jeans, a t-shirt and Converse sneakers. A blue bandana holds her long black hair away from her face.

"Hi, my name is Yasmene. What's yours?"

"Sara. Nice to meet you. How did you know I was in here?"

"I saw what happened. I was in the bunk next to you. Vicky shouldn't have taken your picture. She's sorry, but she'll never tell you that. She doesn't think before she says things. How long ago did your parents die?"

"A few weeks ago."

"Wow, they didn't give you a lot of time to grieve , did they? When I lost my mom, my tía let me stay home for two months before she sent me off to work in the cannery. I couldn't stand that, so I came here. It's not so bad once you get used to it. My mom died last year, I never knew my dad."

"Are you Mexican? You speak a lot of English."

"Yes, I'm Mexican but you can say I've grown up here. I grew up very fast."

"Will you teach me English? I want to learn, I don't understand a lot. I studied it in Mexico but we didn't speak much. We read a lot of books."

"Sure I'll help you. Let's go back to the room. You'll want to meet everyone. It's easier if you know everybody."

I follow Yasmene down the hallway and I am a little relieved now I met someone new. When we enter the room all of the women stop talking and look at me.

"Hey, this is Sara. She's new and she's sad. Let's help her out everybody. She speaks a little English but she wants to learn."

All of the women come towards me to introduce themselves.

"Hola, soy Rosa, I'm from Michoacan. It's my second summer here. It's not too bad, you get used to it."

"Hola, soy María Elena. También soy de Michoacan, I'm Rosa's cousin."

"Soy Isabel, Bienvenida Sara. Are you all alone here? Don't worry we are like family here."

"Debora, me llamo Debora. Isabel es mi Mamá. It's my first time here. I'm afraid too."

"Aren't you going to say anything Vicky?" asked Yasmene.

"Sorry I grabbed your picture Sara, I didn't know about your parents."

I look at the other women and smile, "Tengo miedo pero ya no tanto. I am still a little afraid."

Isabel comes over and hugs me. "Don't worry, Sara. We will help you."

"Lets go to dinner, you'll meet more people there. Are you hungry? ¿Tienes hambre?"

"Yes, I am hungry. I need to speak English. Can I practice with you? ¿Está bien?"

"Of course," They all answer in unison. I turn to finish making my bed and notice it is already made. On top of my pillow someone left the picture of my family with a small teddy bear next to it.

"It's for you Sara. We don't want you to be so sad," Isabel says.

"Gracias, muchas gracias. I am happy to be here with you." The women walk to the dining hall. I follow them and begin to feel a part of the group. As we enter the dining room I see five large tables with benches. At one table a group of men are already eating. Many of them wave and say hello to the women as they walk by.

I see Teodoro and Miguel are sitting with the group of men. They both say hello to the group of women and then smile at me.

"¡Ohhhhh, Sara ya tienes admiradores! Teo and Miguel te están mirando. Look how they are looking at you." Vicky says.

I blush and say, "No they helped me on the boat and in the van. They are nice to everyone I think."

Isabel smiles and says, "Whatever you say Sara. Whatever you say."

Yasmene takes me through the line and shows me what to eat and what to avoid, "Of course the fish is fresh and very good. But avoid the fish stew on Saturdays. It is from the leftovers and it tastes very bad"

"Very bad! You don't want to eat it."

"The pasta is great and the desserts are fantastic here. We have a baker and all of the desserts are made fresh every day. We also have great bread. The one thing we don't have is tortillas. I mean we do have tortillas but they are not good. We need a good Mexican cook."

"I could do that, I make great tortillas," I blurt out.

"Yeah, that would be great but they hired you to work in the fish processing. They aren't going to let you cook. But that would probably be a great job."

Yes, I'd like to work in the kitchen and not work in the fish room. Could that be a possibility? Maybe I won't have to work with fish.

Yasmene and I sit down at the table with the other women and everyone starts talking about the schedule for the following day.

"Tomorrow we start the schedule. Tonight is probably the last night we will all have dinner together. Once the schedule starts we alternate shifts, some of us will be sleeping while others are working."

I hear them talking about the schedule of work six hours on and six hours off. I turn to Yasmene to ask but she is already telling the others a story. I pick up my tray and walk toward the dish room to leave it like I see others do. After leaving my tray I turn to walk back to the table but Teodoro is behind me.

"¿Cómo estás Sara? Te están tratando bien las muchachas?"

"Hola Teodoro, sí estoy bien. They are showing me everything."

"That's great, if you have any questions please ask me. I'd be glad to help."

"Yes, what is six on and six off, no entiendo."

"Ah, sí. That means you work for six hours, take six hours off then go back to work again. So, most people work six hours then go to sleep for six hours."

"When do you eat?"

"It depends, you can eat when you finish your six hour shift, or you can wait."

"Wait? Why would I wait if I am hungry?"

"You'll see Sara, the first couple of days will be easy, but after that you are going to be very tired. You will want to sleep rather than eat."

"De veras?"

"Yes, Sara. You will want to sleep most of the time. Even on your days off. Don't worry."

Yasmene arrives at that moment and says, "What are you telling Sara, Teodoro?

"Nada Yasmene, he is explaining what six on six off means." I say.

"Ah, bueno. Sara you will get used to it. I just found out you will be in the same group as me. I'll help you."

"We work 3 days on that schedule and then we shut down for 24 hours to clean. Everyone works a shift that day to clean, then we get 24 hours off. During that time you can do whatever you want."

"Every three days? That doesn't sound too bad."

"You'll see, Sara, in 24 hours you will work 12 hours and you only have 12 hours left to sleep, eat and everything else."

"Teodoro, tell her what happens if you miss a shift."

"Sí, you will be working a total of 18 hours that day. They take away one of your 6 hour breaks if you miss a shift."

"Is that legal?" I ask before thinking.

Both Yasmene and Teodoro laugh, "Legal? They can do anything here. What are you going to do, swim home?"

Yasmene smiles, "Don't worry Sara, we will help you. We all work together. They are good to you if you do the work. Let's go get some sleep, we need to start work in less than 6 hours."

"Hasta luego Teodoro. Gracias por tu ayuda."

"Hasta pronto Sara. Qué descanses."

We walk back to our room. I'm worried about the work schedule and want to ask one more time if I could work in the kitchen. But, it seems almost an impossible thought if no one else is allowed to change. As I change into my pajamas I glance over at the picture of my family. How could things change so drastically for me in a moment? I climb into bed and turn to face the wall, I don't want the others to see my tears.

"Buenas noches, Sara."

"Buenas noches, Yasmene."

CHAPTER 18

The alarm wakes me from a sound sleep. At first I don't remember where I am, my first thoughts are to roll over and go back to sleep for 5 more minutes and wait for the smell of my mother's tortillas to wake me up.

"¡Sara! ¡Despiértate! We only have ten minutes to get down to the line for training."

Here we go, my first day of working at Fish Camp. I have no idea why they call it that because we aren't at camp, but we can smell fish everywhere we go. I get dressed as fast as I can and follow Yasmene down the long hallway to our work area. Others are walking in the same direction and I hope we aren't late for our first day.

The door opens and I feel the cold as soon as I enter, it's like we've walked into a freezer. It is a freezer; everyone here is wearing a large hooded parka, a woolen hat and large gloves. Someone hands me a large green coat, a pair of work gloves and a hat. I put it on right away to stop shivering. We line up around a conveyor belt and wait for everyone to get their winter clothes on.

The new workers look shocked and I am more shocked than anyone. I never expected to work inside a freezer, everyone failed to mention this fact. A loud voice starts booming from behind us.

We turn to see a slender blonde woman with caterpillar eyebrows shriek, "Let's get this show on the road!"

Some of us start to whisper to the person next to us and we all look concerned.

"Let's stop the jibber-jabber right now! We are here to work, not to meet our new best friend. I want each of you to choose a partner next to you. Don't go running around to find someone you like, look to your left and that person is your partner," the woman barks.

I look to my left to see a timid, dark-haired girl smile at me. I say hello and shake her hand but she doesn't respond.

"My name is Sara, what is yours?" I ask.

No response, just a smile and shaking of her head. Great, my partner is either deaf or doesn't speak English or Spanish. I wonder what language she speaks? By her dark hair and indigenous facial features she appears to be from a rural part of Mexico or Guatemala. I wait for instructions from the boss and worry I won't be successful with my partner. All around me I see people pairing up, chatting and smiling. My partner is smiling but no communication what so ever.

"Okay, now find the two people in the group to your right. This is your work team for this week. The two next to me on the right are people I've never met before but at least they speak English. We move into a group and we are instructed to find a table to sit down. The nearest table is in the back of the room, now I see I should have placed myself near the front, but too late now. The two others appear to be wide awake and ready to begin, but I worry about my partner. She doesn't seem to be listening or know anything that is happening around her.

One of our group says, "Her name is María, she doesn't speak English or Spanish. We haven't been able to communicate with her. She is in our dorm room. But, I think she has a brother who works here."

I turn to her and say, "Hola, Maria. Me llamo Sara."

"Sí maestra, gracias," She says with a smile.

Then I try English, "Hi Maria. My name is Sara. How are you?"

"Si maestra, gracias," she repeats.

"Well, I think you are right. No Spanish or English. Do you think she speaks a dialect?" I ask.

"Must be, we haven't heard her say anything since yesterday. But we did see her with her brother. You may want to speak with him."

We find out our boss is called Debbie and she tells us if one of our group can't keep up the rest of us will have to stay behind to finish. We can lose our break because of someone in our group.

The other two women in my group look over at me and say, "That's not fair, but let's see how it all works. My name is Sandra and this is Alejandra, or Alex for short."

"Nice to meet you, let's see what we need to do next. Are you both new too?"

"Yes, this is our first time, we are new like you, but we think we can work with you well. You seem to be able to follow instructions. We're not sure about Maria."

Debbie yells out some instructions and tells us all to open the boxes on the table. Alex reaches over and opens it up. Inside there are face masks, warming packets for our hands and extra socks. It looks like our days in the freezer are about to begin.

"Everyone take five warming packets and put them in your parka pocket. Then take five face masks and put them in your other pocket," Debbie instructs.

Alex counts out five of each item for us and passes them around the table. The three of us grab the items and put them in our pockets as instructed. Maria stares at me and looks down at the packets in front of her. She has no clue what to do.

I stand up and point to my pockets and show her how to put five of the masks in her right pocket and five of the warming packets in her left pocket. She follows my motions and does what I show her. First communication issue solved.

"The face masks are to use when you are working on the fish saws. You don't want to breathe in frozen particles of fish. Make sure when you are working on that station you are wearing a mask. If I see you working there without a mask you will lose part of your break. Does everyone understand?" Debbie smiles an insecure smile.

The group answers with a roar of, "Yes."

Maria doesn't even notice she was asked a question. Each group has a turn learning how to use the fish saw. As our group approaches the saw we all reach in to our pockets to get a face mask to put on. Maria follows us to the saw, but doesn't put on her mask.

Debbie stops the saw and turns to the three of us with our masks on, "What are you going to do about your team member? She isn't prepared to be near the fish saw. Go back to your table and explain to her what to do. When you are ready come back over. Next group come on over, this group isn't ready," She yells.

We walk back to our table with Maria behind us. I gently push her to sit down and point to her eyes and then to myself. We might as well speak in English and start teaching her English words. I tell the other two to stand up and demonstrate with me. We all reach in our pocket to take out a face mask. We show her and then ask her to stand up and do the same thing. She smiles and stands next to us and pulls out her mask. All four of us put the masks on together. I think she knows now to watch what we do and to do exactly what we do. We do a little happy dance and clap as a group.

She imitates us and smiles, "Gracias maestra."

Now to show her I'm a teammate and coworker, not her teacher. But, in a way I guess we are her teachers. I don't want to be in the role of teacher, but for her safety and ours we will have to demonstrate everything. We are the last group to be trained on the fish saw. The frown on Debbie's face tells me she is going to be impatient with everything we do. She starts by asking Maria to be the first one to learn.

Alex speaks up first and says, "She should go after she watches all of us, she needs help learning."

"She shouldn't be here if she can't do the same work as everyone else," Debbie snarls.

"Maria can do the work, she doesn't speak English or Spanish. She doesn't understand instructions. We'll teach her," I add.

"Okay, Sara you first. Come over here. The rest of you watch."

Debbie starts the saw and shows us how quickly it can cut through your hand by throwing a mannequin arm in the saw. All of the fingers are cut off in a second. She then grabs my hand and shows me where the kill switch is. The saw stops in mid air. She turns around to show everyone where the switch is located. Everyone nods indicating they understand how serious the fish saw is except Maria. She just smiles.

"Okay, Sara you are in charge of training Maria. It's up to you to train her so she doesn't get hurt or cause someone else to die. Understand? It's on you. Now let's move on with the training. Your group is already the slowest group."

How in the world did she just put me in charge of Maria's safety? I'm new too, I can't learn everything and also make sure Maria doesn't get hurt. I look over at Alex and she gestures to me with a thumbs up. I understand that to mean everything will be ok or she will help me. Whatever it means I once again feel overwhelmed with responsibility. I don't want to be an adult, I want to be a seventeen year old on the beach in San Felipe. That isn't going to happen so I need to act like an adult, although it's the last thing in the world I want to do.

Debbie shows us the freezer. Believe it or not there is a freezer inside the freezer room, they call it the deep freeze. After we cut the fish in small portions and pack it in tubs we slide the tubs on a conveyor belt into the freezer. As we walk in to the freezer to learn that part of our training I notice one of the other groups is inside working. Debbie explains to us that we will alternate our groups and spend only ten minutes at a time inside the deep freeze.

The other group looks over at us and I can see in their eyes they hope we are there to relieve them of the cold work. Debbie tells us to ignore them, they have only been in here for five minutes and they have five more minutes to go. We watch as they stack the tubs near a big window. Through the window we can see the tubs have been sent through a small door.

"At this work station you will stack the tubs of frozen fish near the wall over there. See the tubs are marked with dates and time? The tubs are kept here for 4 hours before we send them through the door for packaging. Never send a tub through that has been in here less than four hours. If that happens and you notice you made a mistake you need to notify me right away. We will need to throw that packaged fish away because it may not be thoroughly frozen. We can't sell that to anyone except animal feed companies. Let's hope you never make that mistake. It's always a good idea when you start your ten minute shift in here that two of you double check the bin dates and times. Any questions?"

"Yes, do we wait for the next group to come in, or do we leave after ten minutes?" I ask.

"There is an alarm that automatically tells you when you need to leave, don't stay longer than your ten minutes. It can be dangerous. Understand? Watch to see what happens when the alarm goes off in a minute. This group is almost done."

The alarm sounds and the members of the group look up at Debbie. She motions for them to get out. They drop their last tubs on the conveyor and leave the deep freeze. A new group enters and the alarm resets. She motions for us to move out of the freezer.

"Since we were in there already your group will be next. You can't be in there for longer than ten minutes. Here is a handout to read while you wait," She hands us a plastic covered page and we move back to our table to sit down.

Maria stares at the page and looks up at me. I show her the pictures on the page and tell her to look at them. She glances at the pictures and puts the page down on the table. It's important information about what can happen if we stay in the freezer longer than our assigned ten minutes. Things like disorientation or mental confusion and frostbite. If we feel any of these symptoms we need to go to the medical center right away.

We hear the alarm sound and we stand up to take our turn in the deep freeze. Maria follows every step I take. I signal her to put on her woolen hat and heavy gloves and we enter the coldest place I've ever been in my life. Alex and I check the time and dates on the tubs and make mental note to not go past the fifth stack of tubs.

We make a line and start passing the tubs to each other. We put Maria as the second person in the line so she can see what we do on both sides of her. She does well with this task but I see she is starting to shiver more than the rest of us. I tell her to jump up and down a few times to get the blood flowing through her veins. I look at the clock and see we have two minutes left. Maria is shivering and we have two minutes to go. What should we do? I tell the other two to stop and gather around her in a hug. Maria is surprised but thankful for the protection from the cold. We do this for a minute and then go back to passing the tubs until the alarm sounds. We exit the freezer and Debbie is waiting for us. She looks at us with a questioning look.

"What was that all about, your little hug fest in there?"

"Maria was shivering and we wanted to complete our ten minutes but didn't want her to get any colder," Alex says.

"Whose idea was that?" She asks.

"It was my idea," I say as I raise my hand.

"Good job. You completed your time and got everyone out safely. You need to work together while you are in there."

Alex and I look at each other and smile. At least we

didn't get yelled at on our first shift in the deep freeze, maybe this won't be so hard after all.

"After your shift in the deep freeze you get a fifteen minute break. You can go to the break room next door and get some coffee and take off your gear for a few minutes. It helps you to reset your temperature. Take fifteen and be back on time."

We scramble to get to the break room as fast as we can. Maria is confused by our excitement, but understands when I show her a cup of coffee in the break room. I gesture for her to take off her heavy clothes and enjoy a hot drink. We have completed the first half of our six hour shift and learned three different stations, maybe it won't be too bad.

I inhale the hot, milky coffee and grab a donut from a box on the table. I need calories to keep warm. Maria watches us, but doesn't eat a thing. The box of donuts on the table sits waiting for her to pick any kind of donut you can imagine. I push the box to her side of the table but she smiles and shakes her head. Maybe she thinks she has to pay money. Maybe she thinks they aren't for her, just for us. I grab a donut in a napkin and hand it to her.

She smiles and says, "Gracias, maestra."

I grab a cup of coffee from the urn and bring it to her. I bring milk and sugar to her. She looks at me and mixes the cream and sugar in her coffee. For whatever reason she doesn't feel comfortable enough to serve herself. Maybe in her culture it's impolite to eat without an invitation. I wonder where she is from. Let's hope tomorrow she understands the coffee and donuts are there for everyone and she feels comfortable enough to take what she needs. The fifteen minute break is too short and we return to our next training.

The remainder of the afternoon isn't too bad and we all try to show Maria what to do. Sometimes she catches on right away, other times the blank stare is there with a questioning look. We take turns trying to help her. It helps our group unite to help her. Our shift is almost over and I can't wait to have a shower and rest. I need alone time. It's hard speaking, understanding and teaching in English. Everything I learn I need to reteach to Maria in English. We decided if she doesn't speak Spanish we may as well teach her English.

Each day we begin with a short English lesson for Maria. One of our work team goes to the table where she sits with her brother and personally escorts her to our table. We show her the food, the silverware, the dishes and tell her what they are called. We ask her questions and encourage her to answer. She is beginning to enjoy our company and smiles when she learns something new. By helping her I'm also learning more English. Teaching is the best way to learn.

Debbie notices us in the cafeteria and nods her head as she walks by. It looks like she's happy with us helping Maria. Either that or she feels she has convinced us to do the work she should be doing. We learn to work together in the deep freeze and we have become one of the most efficient teams in that area. There are no prizes for doing a good job, but it's nice to know we are doing well and no one gets hurt.

As the weeks pass by, Maria becomes more comfortable with our group and no longer sits with her brother. I'm not sure if that makes him happy, but I don't care. We all try to help each other survive Fish Camp because we all need each other to make it through the rough days. Each one of us is facing a personal struggle.

CHAPTER 19

A shower will make me feel better. My first thought is take a shower, sleep for a couple of hours and then get something to eat. If I sleep while others are eating it will be quiet in the bunkroom. That's what my plan is, but as I well know my life isn't under my control. I walk down the hall to the shower room and meet Yasmene in the hall.

"Where have you been? I've been waiting for you in the cafeteria."

"I decided to take a shower and sleep a little, then eat later. Isn't that ok?"

"It's ok, but we women stick together. We don't go to our rooms alone and we never go to the shower room alone. We have to watch out for each other."

"Why? What happens? I didn't know it wasn't safe here."

"Don't worry, it is safe most of the time. We know most everyone here in our group, but sometimes some of the workers from upstairs come down to our floor trying to cause trouble. They are nice to us on the work floor, but you don't want to be alone with them. Believe me you need to make sure you stick with the group."

"Yasmene, it sounds like you aren't telling me something. Did something happen?"

"Yes, last summer one of our young girls was harassed by a group of workers from upstairs. She was young and wouldn't listen to our advice. Two guys cornered her and would have hurt her if Miguel hadn't shown up. Miguel told them to leave her alone, luckily they left. Since then we all stick together. Some of them think they can come down here and romance us and we will let them do whatever they want. We know better."

"I'm so glad you told me. You know today when I was working with Maria, she didn't understand things as easily as others. We are teaching her English."

As Yasmene and I walk toward the staff cafeteria Yasmene told me she had heard some of the bosses talking.

"What were they saying?"

"They said you are a great worker and smart. Maybe they'll put you as a leader."

"I don't want that."

"No, you don't understand. If they like you and you do a good job they could ask you to stay on as permanent crew when Fish Camp is over. That would be your ticket to get away from your uncle. You would be able to sign your own contract and earn your own money. Isn't that what you want?" asks Yasmene.

"Yasmene, do you really think they will ask me to stay? I think I'd like to stay just to get away from my uncle. Then I could send more money to my Tía Elena."

I pause to think about what I just said. So many things are running through my head. Will I have to stay alone? Will Teodoro and Miguel be asked to stay too? What about Yasmene?

"What about you, don't you want to stay too? We could work together and …"

"Sara, I don't think they will ask me. I'm not the model worker. The boss on my line doesn't like me. I will probably leave when Fish Camp is over. Unless the Alaska jobs open up, then I'll jump at the chance."

"Alaska, oh no. It has to be so cold!"

"Yes, it is cold but you make a lot of money. They come to pick up a group at the end of Fish Camp. They usually take documented workers but sometimes they will look the other way and let a few people without papers go. That is the ideal job for us because we are away for six months to a year and you can save money. They also will let you go ashore in Alaska and visit some beautiful places. They go in to port every two weeks to get fresh produce and fuel. During those times you can go ashore and go shopping and eat in restaurants. When the job is finished you can go ashore in Alaska and stay there."

"Stay in Alaska? Why would I do that?"

"Think about it, Sara. In Alaska there are very few immigrants from Mexico. You wouldn't have to constantly worry about la migra. Many native Alaskans look like us a little. We'll fit right in. It could be a new start for both of us."

"Wow, it's only my first work day on the ship and already we are making plans to get off the ship. I didn't know all of this was possible. Are you sure?"

"Yes, I know it is possible. I've heard of others doing that. But you have to be prepared to sign on for six months. Do you think you can do that?"

"¡Claro que sí! Of course, anything to get away from my mean uncle and to have freedom to start a new life. Yes, I want to do that! Yasmene, that idea really appeals to me. I've told no one about what Tío Enrique said to me the last time I saw him. Thanks so much for your help." I reach out and give Yasmene a big hug.

"You are like family to me now, the only family I have."

"Let's go get something to eat, our break will be over before we know it."

CHAPTER 20

I worry Maria will be a problem. What if Maria can't do the job right? I'll miss time to rest and eat. There has to be a way to help Maria. At the end of the shift I walk back to the break room with her.

"Maria, do you understand how dangerous the saw is? You work too close to it. I don't want you to get hurt."

Maria smiles and says, "Muchas gracias, maestra"

"I'm not your teacher, I'm your co-worker. Do you understand me?"

"Muchas gracias maestra," answers Maria again. Sí maestra, gracias."

Maria no longer sits with the group in the cafeteria, she now sits with a young man at a separate table. I need to find someone to help Maria understand.

I smile at Maria, "Let's go eat."

Maria and I walk into the cafeteria and Maria goes to sit at her with her brother. I notice the young man is waiting for her. I wonder if he speaks Spanish. I follow Maria to the table.

I hold out my hand and say, "Hola, soy Sara. ¿Cómo te llamas?"

"I'm Humberto, I'm Maria's brother. How was her day?" He says in English.

"Nice to meet you Humberto. It is a little difficult for her. Does she speak Spanish? She doesn't seem to understand me. She keeps thanking me and calling me teacher."

"No, she doesn't. We are from a small village in Michocan and our language is P'urhépecha. Maria never had the opportunity to go to school so she didn't learn to speak Spanish. I am worried she won't be able to do the work, but it looks like she is happy. Thank you for helping her."

"Humberto, she is happy but she doesn't know how dangerous the saw is. I had to tell her two times to be more careful around the saw. She smiles and then does it again a few minutes later. Can you please let her know how dangerous it is?"

Humberto turns and speaks to his sister in a low voice. I wonder if he is embarrassed to speak his native language in front of others. Maria's face changes from a smile to a look of horror.

"What did you tell her?" I ask.

"I told her if she makes more mistakes they will send her home to Tzintzuntzan and she won't be able to stay with me."

"Why would you say that to her? That's not what I asked you to tell her. I want her to know that I will train her but she has to be careful. Can you tell her that please?"

"She needs to know that I'm not always going to be there for her, she has to learn to fend for herself, and learn," Humberto answers.

"How can you be so cruel? She is your sister. Help her. If you don't I will," I say as I walk away.

"I wonder whats happening between those two," Miguel says from across the room.

Teodoro stands up and says, "I don't know, but I'm going to find out. I don't like what I see. Humberto doesn't look like he was very friendly to Sara.

"Hola Sara, what happened with Humberto? Did he give you a hard time?" Teodoro asks.

"He is so rude to his sister. She doesn't speak Spanish or English and he doesn't want to help her. I tried to have him tell her to be careful with the saw. Today she almost got hurt twice and she doesn't understand me."

"I know, Humberto barely spoke Spanish when he first came to Fish Camp. I guess he doesn't remember how difficult it is to not speak the language." Teodoro says.

"Someone has to help Maria, she is on my crew and if we don't do the job right we all lose our break. Oh, by the way Teodoro. Yasmene was telling me about the work in Alaska. What do you know about it? Do you think it is possible I could get hired to go to Alaska?"

"I think you definitely could get hired if you do well here. Miguel and I are talking about going if we can get hired. The work is long hours but you get to go ashore in Alaska and you can even leave the ship and stay ashore. We both like that idea."

"Maybe we can all go together." I say.

Teodoro smiles and says, "I'd really like that Sara. It will be more fun if we have friends to work with and spend our free time seeing Alaska together."

"It seems Mexico is getting further and further away every day. When I think of the ranchito it seems like a lifetime ago. With each day that passes it feels like there are more and more miles between us and Mexico. If we go to Alaska it will be so faraway."

"I know Sara, that's true. But if you surround yourself with good friends it can be almost like family."

"Teodoro, I've only known you a few days and you already are such a good friend. Thank you. You, Miguel and Yasmene are such a great help. It would be great if we could all go to Alaska together. I would feel safer."

"Let's start planning it!" Teodoro says excitedly.

"But what about papeles?" I sigh.

"If you get a recommendation from Mr. G. they will take you even if you don't have documentation. They say they are always willing to take good workers. They know we'll work hard if Mr. G. says he likes us. He is the one you have to impress."

Each day of work seems to roll into the following day without notice. I begin work each shift thinking about how I can get Mr. G to notice me. I see him in passing, but he rarely acknowledges my existence, yet whenever I look up from my work he is watching me from the catwalk above the line. He probably watches everyone, it's just a coincidence that when I look up he is watching me. The work is monotonous and days turn into weeks.

When I enter the cafeteria on the last week of Fish Camp I see the others are gathered in a circle around the bulletin board. This is a first, I've never even noticed the bulletin board until now.

"Qué pasa, Teodoro? I ask.

"Es la lista, Sara. It's the list!" Teodoro answers

"What list?"

"The list of workers invited to continue on the boat to Alaska. Let's look to see if we are on the list!"

Teodoro and I push our way through the crowd and run our fingers down the list.

I quickly spot Teodoro and Miguel's name on the list,

but sadly don't see my own name. It should appear just before theirs, Sara Rodriguez Garcia. But it doesn't appear. I found Teodoro Sánchez Gonzalez and Miguel Sánchez Martin. There is no Rodriguez Garcia on the list.

I back up when I realize I will have to return to live with my uncle again. Miguel and Teodoro are so excited until they notice me sitting at the table by myself.

"Congratulations. I am very happy for you, you are so lucky to be on the list. I guess I won't be going with you," I say with a sad smile.

"What do you mean? Your name is on the list, didn't you see it?"

"Don't kid me Teodoro, it's not funny."

"Didn't you see the list? Come here," Miguel grabs my hand and pulls me to the bulletin board again.

"Look, right here," Miguel points to the list next to the first one.

"Did you read this list? Miguel asks.

I look at the list. At the top of the first list is the word MALE. The second list has the title FEMALE.

"Oh, there are two lists? Male and female? Why would they do that when we all do the same work?"

"It's because they have to tell the next ship how many men and women are coming so they can plan our rooms and accommodations. They usually want half women and half men so there is no question about favoritism. Sara, you are on the list and you are also listed as shift leader, you will earn more money," Miguel says as he hugs me.

I am surprised to be included on the list and even more surprised by Miguel's hug. Over Miguel's shoulder I watch Teodoro turn and walk away. I return Miguel's hug but turn to look at the list one more time. Yes, my name is on the list. Now I wonder what experiences will come my way?

CHAPTER 21

I go through the cafeteria line slowly watching to see if Teodoro returns. I want to sit with him and also want him to know Miguel's hug was unexpected, and also it's not the person I really want to hug. When I watched Teodoro walk away, I realized I have feelings for him. Miguel is nice, but the person I like is Teodoro.

I see Yasmene sitting at the table in the far corner. I grab my tray of food and walk toward Yasmene's table. Yasmene doesn't give me her normal smile.

"Can I eat with you? I haven't seen you in a couple of shifts. Where have you been?"

Yasmene doesn't answer at first. She looks down at her food and tears well up in her eyes.

"I've been sick and Mr. G. took my name off the list for Alaska. I want to work with you. I was looking forward to going, now I have to go home," Yasmene says between sobs.

"I didn't know you were sick Yasmene, I'm sorry. Do you have the flu?"

"Something like that, yeah," the tears continue to fall.

"Yasmene, tell me what's going on, please."

"I'm pregnant."

"What? Are you sure?"

"Well, I wasn't sure until I had to miss two shifts because I wasn't feeling well. Mr. G. sent me to the infirmary, that's why you haven't seen me. The doctor there was suspicious and did a pregnancy test. I'm five weeks pregnant. I want to go to Alaska and start a new life. Now Mr. G. knows I'm pregnant and he took my name off the list," Yasmene's tears continue to roll down her cheeks.

"Yasmene, I don't know what to say? Do you have a boyfriend?"

"Not really, it's complicated. No parents, no boyfriend and now you are going to Alaska without me."

"Okay, tranquila ... let's think about this. Let's make sure you are okay first. Are you feeling better? Can you eat anything? You have to eat. You'll feel better if you eat. Here try some fruit."

"Thanks Sara. I wish we were working on the same line. I never get to see you anymore. I'd feel a lot better if we worked together."

"Maybe I can talk to Mr. G. and request they put you on my line. I guess if he put me on the list for Alaska he must think I'm doing my job. Let me see what I can do. Since you have missed two shifts maybe he will let you join our rotation. He could give you an extra shift off and then you could start with us tonight."

"Sara, that would be great. You are such a great friend."

I'm not such a great friend but I don't tell Yasmene, all I can think about is getting on the next ship, and getting away from my uncle. I'd love to go with her, but her pregnancy will be an issue. I'll help Yasmene as much as I can while we still work together, but I won't give up my own opportunity to move to Alaska with Teodoro and Miguel. I finish my food quietly and think about how I can get Yasmene on my line. I'll ask Teodoro, he will know what to do. Yasmene and I both carry our trays back to the bussing station and walk back to our room. Yasmene is still on sick leave until her doctor appointment tomorrow. We grab our towels and shampoo and go to the shower room.

"Don't worry Yasmene, things will work out. Just try to stay positive."

"Sara. It's not that easy. Things are easy for you."

As soon as the words are out of her mouth she looks down as though she regretted saying that.

"Yasmene, please don't say that. Things aren't easy for me. I miss my family every day. I cry at night when no one is listening. There are days I don't think I can look at one more piece of frozen fish. I may look like things are okay, but believe me, I'm a mess."

"Sara, I'm sorry. I didn't think.... I mean I'm sorry. Please don't be angry with me. I need a friend right now and I'm sorry I said that. You always look like you are doing well and everyone likes you. You make friends easily," Yasmene moves to hug me.

"Yasmene, I am your friend but ... las apariencias engañan. Things aren't always what they seem. Remember that. Let's get finished up here and go get some rest."

"You are right Sara, everyone has something going on in their life that causes them to be sad. We have to move forward and just keep going. Thanks for being my friend."

The grief I feel every day is overshadowed by the exhaustion and frequent queasiness I feel from the constant smell of fish. It is unavoidable, every day no matter how hard I try to wash the smell from my hair and clothes, it is impossible to rid myself of the stench.

I notice some of the others have stopped trying. When in the cafeteria some of the workers wear their fish and blood-stained jackets and don't even bother to leave them on the hook outside the door. I don't know how they can't imagine that others don't want to eat while they sit with their clothes covered in fish scales. Maybe one day I'll reach the point of not caring, but at the moment I still feel the need to remove my work attire and wash up before entering to eat.

Inside our bunk room we have agreed we'll remove our boots and jackets and leave them outside in the hallway. If someone walks through with their boots on we all stare until they get the reminder. It's easy to forget, but not after your bunkmates have shamed you at least once. We take turns cleaning and mopping the floor in our room. Yasmene says some of the other bunk rooms aren't as clean. We all agree we are glad we can get along and keep our area clean.

One day Vicky brought in a sandwich from the cafeteria and left it on her bedside table. It fell behind the table and until the smell of rotten onions reached our nostrils no one knew it was there. The smell wasn't too bad, but bad enough for me to pull out the table to search for an unknown smell.

"Vicky, you can't bring food down here, we'll get bugs." Yasmene says.

"I forgot, somedays I am so tired I can't sit in the cafeteria to eat. I am just too tired. I'm too young to be doing this job, it's not fair. Why do I have to work so hard?" Vicky cries.

Yasmene and I move in to give Vicky a hug. It's hard for all of us, but she is a little younger than us. She accepts the hug and sobs. Yasmene and I look at each other and shrug. The only thing we can do is give her a hug and tell her we know how she feels. We all find ourselves in a give and take situation from one day to the next. Some days we are the ones giving the hugs, other days we receive the them. None of us are where we want to be.

For me it's the grief and loneliness. For Vicky it's the unfairness of her parent's need for her to be the breadwinner and translator for all situations. Not all of the others have shared why they are sad, but there is a general understanding when someone is sad we jump in to be the strong friend for the day. Tomorrow it could be us who needs the extra boost.

Now with the news Yasmene tells me I know she will need a lot of extra hugs and friendship. What can I do to help her?

My work team is close and very supportive also. Since we work together to make sure Maria is okay we watch out for each other too. The teamwork helps pass the time and if we have each other's back we don't worry as much when we are on shift. Sometimes one of us will be extra tired and need more help. We take turns when needed. Because of my friends and co-workers my days become a little less stressful and lonely. My grief is still there, but I can forget about it for a few hours when I am with friends.

When we return to our bunks I see a letter on my dresser. I never get any mail, I don't think my Tía Elena knows where to send me a letter. Today there is a white envelope with black fingerprints on the outside, it is addressed to me. When I pick it up I know it can't be good news, it's from my uncle. Why would he write to me? It can't be anything good.

Sara,

You only have a short time left at Fish Camp until to

come back here with us. When you get back here you can pay towards your coyote, he calls almost every day asking for money. Work hard to see if they'll give you a bonus.

Sometimes they give bonuses to those who work real hard. Oh, another thing, your Tía Elena is sick. She asked me not to tell you. Doctors say there is nothing more they can do for her. She doesn't have long to live.
We are going to be your only family now, you will have to do what we tell you to do.
Hasta pronto,
Tu Tío

I crumple the letter and force it in to the pocket of my work pants. Tears run down my cheeks. I try to leave the bunk area but Teodoro is standing in the hallway waiting.

"Eh Sara, I was going to ask… pero qué pasa?
Sara, what's wrong? Why are you crying?" Teodoro asks as he folds me into his arms.

"My uncle just sent a letter. My aunt is sick and won't get better. She doesn't have long to live."

"Which one? The one in Woodburn or in San Felipe?"

"San Felipe, the only nice family I have left."

"I'm so sorry to hear that Sara, I am really sorry."

"I'm losing another person I love," I cry into his shoulder.

"Wait, Sara. Maybe it's a solution."

I don't want to move away from Teodoro, but it feels uncomfortable when he says that.

I back away and say, "What do you mean a solution? Why would my aunt's death solve anything?"

"That means your uncle has no hold over you any more. You don't have to give him your pay. If he doesn't pay the coyotes they will go after him, not you."

"But he signed my contract, he will get my money."

"Not if you don't go back. They will pay you when you arrive in Alaska. That's how it works. You won't have to worry about anyone harming your aunt if he doesn't pay. Unfortunately, she is dying but fortunately for you that means he can't threaten you anymore. I'm surprised he told you about your aunt. It doesn't sound like he's very smart for a gangster."

"How do I make sure he doesn't get my money?"

"Let's talk to Mr. G. and let him know what's happening. He will make it work for you."

"Okay, will you go with me? I'd appreciate it if you'd go with me."

"Sure, do you want to go now? I think it is more convincing if you go with tears in your eyes."

"Yes, let's go right now. I don't have to be back on shift until 2 o'clock."

Teodoro walks ahead of me toward Mr. G's office. How did I meet such a caring person. Teodoro is so different from my uncle, and today he hugged me. Teodoro knocked on Mr. G's office door and asked if he had time to help us solve a problem.

"I have about five minutes, so if you make it quick I can try to help."

I step in to the office right behind Teodoro. Mr. G. involuntarily takes in a deep breath. I can see he is staring at me. What is he thinking? Mr G. nods his head in the direction of the two well-used chairs in front of his desk. I hesitate until Teodoro moves toward the chairs. I then sit down next to him.

"Mr. G. we have a request or rather we need some advice. Maybe that is a better way to explain it." Teodoro says in English.

"How can I help you?"

I bet he's thinking we are pregnant and need to get married. He must think all kinds of terrible things about me.

Teodoro coughs and starts to speak, "Mr. G., Sara has a situation and I think I have an idea on how to solve it. I just want to make sure I'm not giving her bad advice. Can you tell us what you think?"

"I'll try, what advice did you give her?"

"Sara came from Baja to live with an uncle in Woodburn. I don't know if you know, but her parents and brother and sister were killed this spring so she went to live in Woodburn with an uncle she didn't know. Sara's uncle is not a good man, he is going to take her money when she goes home and force her to work in a cannery or worse. She plans to go to Alaska, but we have a favor to ask. Her uncle signed her up and he will receive her pay. Is there any way she can get her money before we leave? So it doesn't go to her uncle? She was going to let him take the money but he wrote and said her aunt in San Felipe is dying and Sara will never be able to return to live there. The only reason she wants to go back to Woodburn is to help her aunt. The coyotes told her if she didn't pay with the money she earned here they would hurt her aunt.

I add, "You see I don't have family in San Felipe any more. The only family I have left is in Woodburn and they don't want me there, they only want me to work to help pay for my cousin's college and clean their house. I don't want to go back there and I hope I could get my pay or at least some of it to get a new start in Alaska. Teodoro and Yasmine told me you can get good jobs in Alaska after you finish your job on the freezer ship. I don't want to go back where the only job I can get is in a cannery or live with my uncle. I'd have to worry about ICE all the time. Do you understand?"

Mr. G. turned away from us and looked out over the production floor below.

"I've spoken with your uncle Sara. Teodoro is right, he is not a good person. He wants me to give you overtime so you can earn more money for him. He didn't even ask how you were or if you liked your job. He only asked how he could get more money from your work. I have an idea but you cannot mention it to anyone. Go back to your bunks and get a bag ready for later tonight. You can only take the bare essentials, I don't want anyone asking you what you are doing. Can you do that?"

I look at Teodoro and wonder what we started with this conversation.

Teodoro doesn't look worried and he looks at me and asks, "Is that ok with you Sara?"

I don't answer right away. Slowly, I turn back to Mr. G. and say, "What will we be doing? I don't want to do anything unless I know exactly what to expect."

Mr. G. smiles and says, "What like go on a freezer ship with complete strangers for six weeks? Sara, you have already been through the worst part. Do as I say, go get only what you need. I'll take care of the rest. Leave everything you don't need so others won't get suspicious. Meet me back here at nine pm sharp."

"Okay, but will we be together? I don't want to go alone."

"I wouldn't send you anywhere alone Sara. Teodoro is going with you. But you can't mention it to Yasmene or Miguel even though they are your friends. Can you do that?"

"Yes, I think so," I mumble.

"Of course," said Teodoro.

"See you back here at nine pm on the dot."

"Okay, we'll be here. What if someone asks what we are doing?"

"Tell them you are spending some time alone, like a date. They'll stop asking if you pretend your are sneaking off to be alone."

I blush and Teodoro smiles, "Maybe we are," Teodoro says.

"Before you leave I want to say one thing to you both. Stick together through this. There may be some rumors but that is to mislead your uncle, Sara. Ok?"

"Okay."

We turn to leave and I say, "I won't forget this Mr. G. You are so nice, almost like family."

"I just want you to be safe Sara. I don't like to see any of our young people mistreated by anyone especially their own family. Go get something to eat, grab some fruit and an extra sandwich."

"Ok, we'll be back at nine sharp."

Neither of us say a word as we walk down the stairway from the office. Each one afraid the other one will change their minds.

"Well, I guess we'll get to spend some more time together Sara," Teodoro laughs.

"I guess we will. Are you sure you want to do this? We don't even know what we are going to do."

"Mr. G. must have a plan. He wouldn't put us in danger. He said he would explain it tonight. Go get your bag ready. I'll see you in the cafeteria in 30 minutes. Is that enough time?"

"Yes, more than enough. I don't have a lot to pack. Some pictures and a change of clothes," I lean closer and give Teodoro a hug.

"Thanks so much for helping me. You helped me from the first time I got sick in the van. You are very special to me."

"Sara, you know you are special to me too. Te adoro." He laughs and walks away toward his room.

CHAPTER 22

The only thing I want to make sure I take with me is the picture of my family. But how am I going to take it from my table without Yasmene noticing it. She knows it is always in the same place on the table. I look through my things and decide what to take. I write a note to Yasmene and leave it in her sweatshirt pocket. That way she won't get it until tomorrow when she goes to work.

I grab a change of clothes, my toothbrush and a few other items and stick them in my laundry bag. The laundry bag won't cause suspicion because if anyone asks I can say I need to get some laundry done. At eight forty-five I start to walk toward the door when the last shift of workers walks in.

"Hola Sarita, ¿Qué pasa? ¿A dónde vas?"

"Me? Nowhere. I'm going to take this laundry down to wash. I'll be right back."

I grab my laundry bag and leave before anyone else could ask any questions.

I see Teodoro waiting for me in the cafeteria. I smile, he is very handsome and he is nice to me. I know he likes me. So what is the problem?

"Sara, let's go. It's almost nine. We need to be upstairs."

"Ok, ok. I just got caught up with the last shift coming in when I was leaving."

We both climb the stairs and wonder what is in store for us next.

The lights are turned off but Mr. G says, "Come in and sit down and close the door."

Teodoro and I start to worry. Why are the lights off and what does Mr. G have planned for us? We drop our bags next to the door and sit in front of Mr. G's desk.

"You are both going to disappear tonight. You will be safe but no one will know where you are. I will personally tell them you are ok once you are aboard the next ship headed to Alaska. The reason for all of the secrecy is that I can withhold your pay Sara if you disappear or run away. I don't have to pay your uncle if you don't complete your contract. Of course he thinks there is no way you won't complete it because you are on a ship with no place to go."

"Will he think I'm dead?" I ask.

"He won't know what to think. We have a supply ship coming in thirty minutes. They unload supplies into the kitchen area. There is a cargo door there. You will pretend to hide in the recycling and when they take it to the other ship my friend there will get you and settle you in until you meet up with the other ship headed north. How does that sound?"

"Will there be food and a place to stay? Or do we need to hide?"

"No, my friend Bill will make sure you have a place to stay and food. You should be with them for three days. They go from ship to ship out here with supplies. The last ship they meet up with is heading to Alaska. You will work with them in the kitchen on the way north. It will take about a week. Are you ok with working in the kitchen?"

"I love cooking! I don't mind at all."

"I don't know about cooking but I can wash dishes.," Teodoro says.

"Good, the story is that you two decided to run away together. You can make it true or not, but that is what is happening on this end. I will tell the others you are safe and you left to work on another ship going to Alaska. Which is true. This is for your protection. If you run away Sara, I don't have to pay you."

It's hard to hide my disappointment.

Teodoro asks about his pay as well. Mr. G. put his hand up motioning us to stop talking, "You both will get your money. It will be sent to your next ship and they will disburse it to you on the first payday after you arrive. You will need to get a bank account I think, but that will be taken care of later. We need to do it this way so your uncle can't hear from your friends that you escaped with my help. I will deal with him, if what you say is true he won't look for you. Any questions?"

"Maybe I made a mistake. I left a note for Yasmene telling her I was leaving."

"Did you mention my name or say anyone was helping you?"

"No, I just said because I no longer had to take care of my aunt and I don't want to go live with my uncle I decided to run away."

"Good. She won't know anyone helped you."

"Did you mention Teodoro?"

"No, no I didn't."

"Good."

"What will happen is tonight when you don't show up

for bedtime check, Yasmene will let us know you are missing. Or if she reads the note first she may wait til morning to let us know. By then you will be on the supply ship heading off to deliver food to the other ships. Any questions?"

"No, well yes. Will they keep us together? I mean will we stay together all the way to Alaska?"

"Yes, there is no reason to separate you. In a week's time when the others head to Alaska they will be surprised to meet up with you again. You can then tell them the whole story, or not. Up to you. Ok let's go through my secretary's office, it leads down a different stairwell. It is just a few steps from the kitchen." Mr. G. opens the door and we follow him into the darkness.

Before going through the door Teodoro turns to me and says, "Are your sure you want to do this?"

I answer yes by leaning in and giving Teodoro a kiss on the lips, "As long as we can stay together I'm ok with this."

Teodoro smiles, grabs my hand and we both walk down the long, dark narrow hallway behind Mr. G. My eyes take a few moments to adjust to the darkness. I hold on tightly to Teodoro's hand. I'm too afraid to let go. It must be the nerves I think to myself. Teodoro hasn't said a word since we started down the hallway. He held my hand tightly but I noticed he was sweating and breathing heavily. Could it be that he was scared too? He always seems so in control. At the end of the hallway there are stacks of tubs with recycling waiting to be offloaded on to the next ship. The doors open and the noise coming from the other ship along with the smell from recycling makes me dizzy. The saltiness of the air and the cold splashes me in the face along with the lights that flash in my eyes.

Teodoro grabs my hand tighter and starts running for the door.

"Wait, slow down Teodoro. What are you doing?" I cry. "Why the rush?"

I am dragged through the stacks of garbage and recycled bottles and my feet can hardly keep up with the pace that Teodoro set. Tears spring from my eyes and I start to fear for my life. Teodoro doesn't seem like the same person. I start kicking and screaming and try to make my body limp like a dead weight. Teodoro keeps pulling on my arm and I am now on the floor trying to wrestle out of his grip. I almost manage to get away when Mr. G. grabs my other hand and pulls me off the floor. Why is Mr. G. pulling on me? What's happening? Have I made the right decision to join Teodoro? Is he the person he said he is? I'm being kidnapped by people I know. I thought I could trust them, but they are going to kidnap me just like the others from the bus station.

"Sara, just hold on, don't let go. Come on, we need to get on the next ship. Hang on!" Teodoro yells as he pulls on my arm even harder.

Mr. G. yells to Teodoro, "Make sure you don't let her get back on this ship, she has to get on that boat."

The motion of the two ships along with the tension of being dragged makes me feel nauseous and faint. The memory of my panic attack in the van comes back to me, now would not be the time to have a panic attack. I am being kidnapped. Negative thoughts flood my mind. My eyes are watering and sweat pours from my body. I collapse and am carried on to the next ship.

I wake up in the infirmary. I'm not sure who put me here or why Teodoro and Mr. G. acted the way they did. I'm terrified.

Teodoro walks over to sit next to me. He starts to take my hand but I pull away.

"Teodoro, I don't know what you have done. What is this? Why did you and Mr. G. do that? I am so scared. I thought we were going to Alaska. What happened? Where am I?"

My mind starts to wander back to the accident that changed my life. Why is everything so difficult? For the past few weeks since the accident nothing has been the way I imagined it could be. I hear a voice in the hallway that reminds me of my little sister. The voice is so familiar and the tears start to roll down my cheeks again. This is all too difficult.

The door opens and Diana, my younger sister, walks in the door followed by my mother and father. A few minutes later Diego, my brother, runs in and shouts, "Sara, te he echado de menos!"

A doctor is behind them and I hear myself shrieking. I feel like I'm going crazy. This has to be a nightmare. First I feel like I am being kidnapped, now a vision of my family appears before me. I must be going crazy. The doctor comes toward me with a needle and the woman who looks like my mother helps hold me down while he gives me an injection. That's the last thing I remember.

My face is wet from tears when I wake up in my mother's arms, "Hija, todo está bien, no te preocupes."

Is this a dream? How can my mother be here with me on the ship? Teodoro is here, my family is here and it's not possible. It has to be a dream, or was everything else a nightmare?

I can't speak, I can't think, I am so overwhelmed and my body is frozen with fear. It's like a nightmare where you can't wake up. Someone wraps me in a blanket and my mother pulls me closer. She is hugging me so tight I can't breathe. My brother, Diego, is also hugging me. Diana is behind my mother and tears run down her cheeks. When I sit up I see my father with his face in his hands sobbing.

"Papá, eres tú? I can't believe you are all here, I can't believe it. I don't want to believe it and find out it's a dream."

"It's not a dream, Sara," Teodoro assures me.

"We are all real, mija. We're here with you," Papá says.

"Give me a minute. I don't understand at all. How are you here? They told us you were all dead.

"We will explain it all to you. First, the ship doctor wants to look you over. I'll show you to the clinic area on the ship. Your parents can come with you, I think the rest of you should go to the cafeteria and wait for us there. How does that sound?" Teodoro. says.

"Can my brother and sister come with us? I don't want to be separated again."

"Sure, I don't think that's a problem. Let's go."

My dad leans down to pick me up, my arms go around his neck and I don't want to ever let go. I don't know how this happened but I don't want to worry about it now. I have my family back and that's what matters.

The doctor checks me over and prescribes some tranquilizers and sleeping pills in case I need them. I don't want to take any pills and possibly go back to the reality that was yesterday. My mother thanks the doctor and puts the pills in her pocket. She smiles for the first time. I'm not sure if I can smile yet, the tears get in the way. The doctor tells me I may experience some flashbacks or panic attacks, if I do I can take one of the tranquilizers to help me through it. I am eager to get the details and want to go to the cafeteria with the rest of the group. No one is telling me anything.

"Hija, are you sure you are strong enough to sit with the group? Maybe you should rest."

"Papá, I've been strong enough to cross the border by myself and travel over twelve hundred miles on a bus. I think I can sit with a group and get some kind of explanation."

"You're right. You are so brave and I'm so sorry you had to do this. It was the only way."

"I want to hear every detail. I want to know everything."

"We'll tell you everything. Believe me these past two months have been agony for us, we didn't know if you were safe or not, didn't know if you would make it. You are so strong."

Diana blurts out, "Papá, do you think the FBI was watching Sara the whole time?"

"Not now, Diana. Not now."

"What? What about the FBI?"

CHAPTER 23

The cafeteria is filled with people. Why are all of these people here? I have so many questions. I see the doctor has also joined us. Why would he be involved? Teodoro hands me a café con leche and pulls out a chair for me. I motion for my parents to sit next to me. Diana and Diego scoot chairs over to be near us. Someone hands me some toast and jam to have with my coffee and I realize I am starving.

My first bite of toast almost falls from my mouth when I see Patty and John walk through the door. Confusion and anger well up inside of me. Who tells the truth anymore? Who can I trust?

Patty walks over and leans in for a hug, "Sara, will you forgive me?"

"I don't know, I don't understand anything. Why are you here? Where is your baby?"

"It will take us a while to explain everything. The first thing I need to tell you is I am an agent with the FBI, John is too."

"So, you followed me? You didn't just run in to me? It was all a lie?"

"We were given an assignment to protect you from the minute you were in the States. Before that the federales were watching you."

"What about Samuel and Esmeralda? Were they protecting me too?"

"No, that was the dangerous part of the operation, you were being watched, but anything could have happened until you were dropped off at the bus station in Caléxico. Once there, I was able to get close to you and monitor your safety."

"What about the two men who tried to kidnap me in the bus station?"

"Well, no they weren't part of the plan. They were part of the pipeline we were trying to bust. Let me start from the beginning."

"Wait. Papá, when did you get involved? What about the accident? Was that planned? Patty, I need for my father to tell me how this started."

My father gets a serious look on his face and says, "It was just as much a surprise to us as it was to you. If you had been with us it would have been so much easier. I had no idea when we left you in San Felipe what was about to happen. We were stopped at a military control when the federales approached us. We were more or less kidnapped on the spot, but for our own safety. We were taken to a safe house in Tecate to wait. They made up the story about the accident. It was brutal knowing you were on your own and full of grief. We were given an option of giving our help or we would be let go. They told us of the children who are trafficked in a pipeline along with drugs from Baja all the way up the I-5 corridor. Your mother and I argued about whether we should help out and possibly put you in danger or not help out and feel the guilt each time a child went missing. The decision to help out wasn't an easy one, but we knew you were strong and the Federales assured us you would be watched the whole way. When they told us you were almost kidnapped in the bus station we were furious."

"I understand a little more now. It was so difficult to think I lost you all. Papá I cried every night. Tía Elena wept so much, she couldn't handle the loss. What about her? Is she really sick?"

"Yes, unfortunately she is ill and won't recover," he says with tears streaming down his face. "There's nothing we can do to change that."

"Wait, but how did you get her to send me to Tío Enrique?" My father hesitates before answering. I can tell he struggles to talk about his sister and the idea of using her when she was sick. Before he answers Patty interrupts.

"Your primo Juan is part of the plan. He is involved in the trafficking pipeline and works for the narcos. We have a mole within his gang who planted the idea of asking for more money from your Tía Elena and then encouraging her to send you north if she couldn't pay. Our target is your Tío Enrique and his associates, including primo Juan. We learned the men who tried to kidnap you in Caléxico are associated with Juan. His gang had plans to kidnap you and send you up the pipeline."

The silence is deadening. No one speaks. A chill sweeps through my body and I reach for my mother's hand. My father puts his arm around my shoulder. I could have been the victim of sex trafficking. I was in a lot more danger than I had ever known.

Patty speaks up, "Sara, the most important thing to remember is that you are safe now. You and your parents have helped the FBI, ICE, Homeland Security and local agencies get some of the big names in the cartel. We are sorry for the pain and suffering you and your family have gone through, but we have some results that are positive."

"Patty, were you ever pregnant? Is John your boyfriend?"

"No, we felt you would feel safer with a pregnant woman, you'd be less afraid to stay close to a mother figure. I befriended you to save you Sara. I needed to get you as far as LA. Did you notice another woman sat with you for the remainder of most of the trip? She is also an agent. The baby is her real daughter. She is one of our bilingual agents with the FBI, we are all bilingual in this department."

"We can explain who everyone is and how they helped as you have more questions. Right now, because you and your family are safe, the FBI, HSI and ICE have moved in on your Tío Enrique and his associates. We have word they have been picked up and are in custody. You helped us make the arrest of more than ten members of his group."

"Oh no, what about his wife Karina, and his kids?"

"If they aren't involved they will be okay. All of your uncle's assets will be taken and their lifestyle will change but they should be ok. José and Natalia were born in the States. We aren't sure about Karina at the moment. They are checking on her. It's possible she has false papers."

"They told me they were all documented and I was the only one without papers."

"Remember hija, las apariencias engañan. Things aren't always as the appear or what they seem. They may have told you that but it doesn't mean it's true."

"What will happen to Karina if she is undocumented? Wait, she was working at the hospital, she must have papers."

"Not really, many immigrants buy what they call a chueca or fake social security card. They can use it for years without getting caught. You probably don't realize the number of people in the States who work with illegal papers. They integrate into the culture, get jobs, their kids go to school and they become americanized and no one suspects they don't have the correct paperwork. That could be Karina's case, but we don't know yet."

"Will her children be penalized?"

"No, but they may be sent to live with another family if the father is in prison and the mother is picked up by ICE."

"Mamá, that's terrible. Can't we help?"

My mother looks down at her hands and then at my father, "No, hija. They can't know we are still alive. We get new identities and will move to a new town to start over. If someone in the cartel finds out we are alive they'll know it was a set up and we were involved. We would all be in danger."

"Poor José and Natalia."

"Were they worried about you?" Patty asks.

"José was, he tried to help me. He told me to come to Fish Camp because he was suspicious of his dad. He didn't know what his new job was but he knew they had more money than ever before. He told me his dad was acting mysteriously."

"We can't worry about them right now hija. We want to make sure you are safe and we want to all be together. If we contact them we will jeopardize our safety. The cartel is nothing to mess with."

"I'm starting to understand. It will take me a long time to process all of this, but I am so happy to have my family back."

"Teodoro, did you know my family was alive?"

"No, Sara. But Miguel and I were asked to watch out for you by Mr. G. He knew we would be in the same van and on the same work crew. He put us together. We didn't know why we were protecting you. Now, it all makes sense. We were happy to watch over you. Mr. G. told me I had to grab you and get you on this ship as soon as possible. That's why I did what I did. I knew something big was about to happen. "

Yasmene says, "I didn't know anything Sara, I knew Teodoro and Miguel were quite careful around you and tried to help you fit in. I had no idea they were protecting you."

At that moment Mr. G. walks in. He. interrupts, "No one else knew a thing. The FBI asked me to watch over you from the time your uncle dropped you off. I knew Teodoro and Miguel would be there and they would make sure nothing happened to you until you were on board the ship."

"How are you involved Mr. G.?" I ask.

My father looks at Mr. G and smiles, "Sara, meet your great uncle. Mr. G. or Mr. Gonzalez is my uncle. He left the ranchito years ago and you never met him, but you had family near you since you boarded the ship. Years ago he was a Federal Police Officer in Baja. When he left Mexico and emigrated to the States he worked with the FBI in the gang division. It's not a coincidence you were sent to Fish Camp, it was all part of the plan. Tío Enrique was led to believe it was his idea to send you here. The idea was carefully planted in his head by another mole we have working in Woodburn."

"You are my uncle? Is that why I felt like you were watching me all the time?"

"Well, yes I was watching you because you are family but also because you are a good worker. I wasn't told until this week that your family was still alive. I knew we were trying to get your Tío Enrique, but I thought the story of the accident was true. It was best for all of us. It would have been difficult for me to keep that a secret."

"But Teodoro and I came to you to ask your advice. How did you know we would do that? We didn't even know we would ask for your help until I got the letter from Tío Enrique."

"A lot of the details fell in to place, but we weren't sure how this part of the operation would take place. Let's just say Teodoro was told to encourage you to reach out to me for help. Your uncle's letter just happened to arrive on the right day. The news of your aunt's illness freed you up to leave for Alaska. Your Tío Enrique's greediness pushed you to make the decision to leave. If you hadn't come to me asking for advice I was going to send you ahead to help on the supply ship, that's why I made you a shift leader. So you wouldn't be suspicious. You and Teodoro would have gone ahead of the group."

"Patty, were you in a black SUV in the Safeway parking lot that day? Was that John with you?"

"I knew you were too smart for us. You saw us and I had to duck down and pretend I dropped something. Yes, it was us. We watched you each time you left the house and walked to Safeway. When you were pushed down with the groceries it was one of Tío Enrique's crew trying to get your attention. We think they planned to kidnap you that day, but those two men were too quick to help you. They work for us."

"Was Tío Enrique going to kidnap me and sell me to the traffickers?"

Once again there wasn't a sound to be heard in the room. Patty looked at Mr. G., then my father and mother.

She struggled to get the words out, "Yes, we think he planned to kidnap you and sell you to the traffickers. Our presence there in the parking lot was a safety precaution, but it may have saved your life."

The reality of the danger I had been in hit me hard. I was making food, doing the laundry and sleeping in the house of a cruel sex and drug trafficker. The bile rose in my throat and I stood to run to the rest room. I barely made it to the door when I vomited all over the floor. Beads of sweat rolled down the back of my neck and I started to get dizzy. Teodoro and my father picked me up and carried me to one of the bunk rooms. Diana helped pull open the covers of the bed and they placed me in bed.

Teodoro took off my tennis shoes and placed them under the bed. My mother got some cold towels and placed them on my forehead. It was too much. The grief was terrible, the fear of ICE and kidnappers was terrible but the thought that my own uncle would have sold me to sex traffickers left me without air to breathe. I started to hyperventilate and the doctor came in to check on me. Before I knew it he had given me a shot and I drift …

CHAPTER 24

My eyes blink open and I sit up. Where am I? My mother is asleep in the bed with me, next to us is my father on one bunk and Diego and Diana on another. They are really here. I can't believe it, it wasn't a nightmare, they are here. However surreal, they are here.

I reach for my shoes under the bed and have a flashback of what happened last night. So much information, so many people and from what I remember quite a bit of vomit. My stomach rumbles and I need to get some food. I tie my shoes, slip off the bed and cover my mother with the blanket. What my parents must have gone through while waiting to reconnect with me! I can only imagine it may have been equal to or more than the grief I experienced.

This new ship is smaller than the freezer ship but still big enough to get lost. I wander for a few minutes before I see some stairs and sign indicating Galley. The stairs are a short walk to reach the cafeteria. When I enter I see Teodoro sitting by himself with his head in his hands.

"What's wrong? Are you okay?"

"Sara, I'm so glad you feel better. Come sit next to me and I'll get you a coffee and some breakfast."

"I think I'll accept your offer. I still feel a little queasy," I say as I sit down.

"No problem, I'll get your coffee first. Be right back."

Whether or not Teodoro lies, or tells half-truths I'm not sure. One thing I'm sure of is that I am glad he is watching out for me and I'm glad he's still here. I hope we can stay friends and maybe more.

My cafe con leche appears in front of me with a sweet roll.

"Here, this will hold you until I get you some real breakfast. What would you like?"

"I'd love bacon, eggs, hash browns and toast. Bacon extra crispy please."

"Coming up right away."

The dark sweet liquid of the cafe con leche soothes my throat and stomach. I didn't realize how hungry I was. The sweet roll dipped in the coffee is even better. I can't wait to get the rest of my breakfast. I look over to see Teodoro watching me, when he notices he turns his head to the side as if pretending to be looking at something else. I know he was looking at me.

Maybe he likes me as much as I like him. The plate of breakfast is put on the table, I grab my fork and knife and dig in. I'm ravenous. The eggs, bacon and potatoes taste great along with the toast and jam. I may need another cafe con leche but don't want to ask Teodoro to bring me anything else. Before I know it, he has brought his plate of breakfast to sit next to me and a second cafe con leche for me. He is so sweet. I think. Maybe I need to be more cautious.

"Thank you, it's very nice of you to bring me my food. I'm feeling better already."

"You look better, I was very worried last night. You looked like you were in shock."

"I think I probably was. It was a lot to take in. But I'm better today. I think the doctor gave me something to sleep."

"Yes, he gave you a shot and you fell asleep right away. I was so worried about you."

"How much did you know? Did you know any of that?"

"No, the only thing I knew is that Mr. G. asked us to watch out for you. He said you had lost your family and needed some friends. He wanted to make sure no one took advantage of you. He did tell me to take you to him if any situations came up where you needed help. Yesterday he told me to get you on that ship asap even if I had to drag you on. That's why I started running. I was afraid you'd change your mind."

"It's so strange to find out Mr. G. Is my dad's uncle, and he was in the FBI. Could you imagine working for the FBI? Wouldn't that be cool?"

"Sara, are you already planning your future. You need to take one day at a time, rest up and get strong again."

"Just dreaming. Now that I know what awful things are done to young children and teenagers, I want to help stop the possibility of trafficking. It could be a goal. I know I don't even have papers but it would be great to work with the FBI".

"Who wants to work for the FBI?" Patty asks as she enters the cafeteria.

"Hi Patty, we were just talking how it would be so cool to help stop those traffickers."

"You both have already helped do that. Everything you did helped us put away some heavy hitters. It will put a clog in their pipeline for a while."

"I'm worried about José and Natalia. Even Karina because I don't think she knew what was happening. She seemed very stressed."

"Well, John and I are headed back to Seattle tonight. We will let you know what happens to them if we can. In the meantime I need to know if you have any information you can share about what you observed at your Tío Enrique's house. You don't have to do it now, but I'd like to know before we leave the ship tonight."

"That's okay, I do have some information and I have to admit to something I did. I think I need to turn it in to you because I don't want to be a part of the investigation."

"Let me get John and we'll listen together. You finish your breakfast and I'll be right back."

"I have some evidence in my backpack if you need it."

"Of course, but right now just give us a rough idea of the information. I'll be right back."

When Patty and John return I begin my story, "Three hundred dollars, I took three hundred dollars of Tío Enrique's money. I have it in my backpack. I want to return it now."

"Sara, hold on. How did you take money from him? Did he leave it around the house or what?"

"In his pockets I found fifty thousand dollars. At first I just left it on top of the dryer in a tray along with a small plastic baggie. He came home one morning and ran upstairs searching for his money. He started yelling at me and asking where his jeans were. He said I was nosey because I found what was in his pockets, he yelled at me and took the money and left. That was the first time."

"There was a second time?"

"Yes, the same thing happened. I put his clothes in the washer. When they came out of the dryer I found another wad of fifty thousand dollars in a rubber band. This time I took three hundred dollars and left the rest in an envelope he told me to use. He told me to put it in the garage. I don't think he wanted Karina to know how much money he had."

"I took the money because he wasn't nice to me and I thought I might need it if they kicked me out of their house. When I left I also took a pair of my cousin's tennis shoes, a jacket and a dress. She has so many she'll never notice. But, now I feel bad and I'll return them."

"Anything else?"

"Yes, one day he came home and asked me to help take some seats out of a big passenger van. I had to release the seat while he lifted. I guess he couldn't do it without help. When I lifted up the one seat a picture of a little girl fell out. I picked it up and put it in my pocket. A few minutes later I found a note. The note said, Ayudame, or help me. It was scribbled in pencil on a piece of paper."

"Do you still have the note and the picture?"

"Yes, and I saw the little girl from the picture in the newspaper. She was reported missing in Woodburn. I think my Tío Enrique kidnapped her in his van. I wanted to go to the police but I was afraid ICE would pick me up. José told me stories of ICE picking up undocumented people in Woodburn and deporting them. He said they don't deport you to your hometown, they leave you at the border where the narcos can pick you up. I didn't want that to happen so I didn't go to the police, sorry. I should have helped that little girl."

"Because of what you did you helped more than one little girl. We hope we can find the girl in the picture, sometimes if we help find one child it isn't enough. We need to stop the pipeline. You helped do that."

"All the people I saw along the way with those reflective sunglasses were watching me?" I ask.

"You are very observant, yes they were watching you."

"I guess it helps to know I was being watched over, but it still scares me to think what could have happened. Why are Yasmene and Miguel here? I thought Yasmene's name was taken off the list because she's … I mean her name was taken off the list."

"I'll let her tell you her story. Yes, Yasmene is pregnant. She won't be going to Alaska, she'll be going to a new town just like your family. She will also be in witness protection."

"Why, I don't understand?"

"Yasmene also has some evidence and information about the trafficking pipeline. I don't want to give you too many details because it's private, but she may share with you if she wants."

"What happens to my family now? We can't go back to San Felipe or the ranchito in Baja. Where will we go? Will ICE pick us up? Will we be safe in Alaska?"

"You are very persistent. I wasn't going to explain it to you until later. Your parents already know so I might as well tell you. You are all covered under the Witness Protection Act. That means you can never contact friends or family or anyone you knew before going to Fish Camp. Even some people in Fish Camp won't be allowed to know where you are."

I glance at Teodoro and think that we'll be separated. I don't want that, I want to get to know him better.

Patty noticed my questioning look and answered, "Teodoro will also be included in the program, as will Miguel and Yasmene. Whether or not you will be placed together is a big question. It's not up to me."

"Can we still communicate?" Teodoro asks.

"Not unless you are placed in the same town. It's rare that we do that but it's possible. I think the best advice to give you is to ask a lot of questions. When we get off in Seattle another agent will come aboard with the WITSEC program. They are Federal Marshalls, they do the placements and relocations. Talk to your parents Sara, see how they feel."

"Teodoro, I don't want to be separated, do you?"

"No, Sara. I don't. Let's ask to be placed in the same town."

"What about ICE? How will we live, work or go to school?"

"Well, that's the good news. First, you will be given a place to live and enough money to pay your rent etc. They will help you find jobs or schools. The best news is you will receive legal residency. Your papers are being processed now. You will have new names, passports and social security cards. You will be legal."

"What? Do my parents know that? Have you told them that?"

"When we all get together we will give you all the details and choices you have to make."

"Will we be together?"

"We won't separate your family, no."

"Teodoro is now part of my family, Yasmene and Miguel too. I hope we can all be together. They helped me survive my time at Fish Camp. There is no way I could have survived these past few weeks without them. Will we be able to stay together?"

"That depends on the WITSEC agent. They know all of the restrictions and rules, we need to wait for them to come aboard."

"I don't want to be separated from them, they are my family too."

"We understand Sara, really we do. But there are rules, like I said we have to wait to talk to the agent in charge of your placement."

Thoughts invade my head. Why is everything so difficult? I'm reunited with my family for 24 hours and now I may lose my friends and never see them again. More than that, I don't want to lose touch with Teodoro. I know that for sure. I won't give any more information to the agent until I know we can stay together.

"I'm not leaving without them, Patty. They are my family now. I won't agree to anything if they can't come with us," I cry and stamp my foot.

"Teodoro, let's go find my parents. Patty, we'll be back with the rest of my family."

"Wait Sara, John and I will be leaving and I don't want to say goodbye to you like this. I won't be able to contact you once you enter the program. Can we end this as friends?"

"Sorry, Patty. I know I'm being selfish but I've been through so much and I want to be able to make some decisions. I've been in the dark for so long, my world was turned upside down and now everyone expects me to just start a new life and start over. I won't leave my friends behind. Thank you for your help. I appreciate all you've done for me. Will we never see each other again?"

"That's how it works. You leave your old life behind, all acquaintances and friends. In your case you will have to ask the agent to help you. There may be some exceptions. But I don't want to promise anything."

"At least you helped me get this far. I'll miss you and your baby, " I say with a smirk.

CHAPTER 25

Yasmene walks toward me and asks me to sit down with her, alone. Teodoro looks at me as if to ask if I'm okay alone. I nod yes and he walks away. I know he won't be far away.

"Sara, there were so many things I wanted to tell you. We became friends so quick and I wasn't able to tell you the truth. I'm sorry about that. My life took a turn for the worse when I came north from Mexico. Remember I said I lived with my aunt? That's a lie. I'm alone here like you. I have no one left either. That's why your friendship is so important to me. Please listen to my story before you ask any questions, okay?"

"Sure, I'm ready to listen. What happened?"

"I left Mexico like you. I had no one left, the narcos killed my family. A neighbor helped me find a coyote to come north. He wasn't a nice man. Things happened."

"What kind of things, Yasmene?"

"I was smuggled across in the back of a truck with fifty others, there was hardly room for us to sit down. It was a delivery truck packed with furniture, that only left space enough for us to sit or lie on top of the furniture, there wasn't a lot of air, no food and no bathroom stops. You can imagine how we arrived in Arizona. Once we arrived, we were separated and placed in smaller vans. Each van held fifteen dirty, smelly people. You can't imagine the stench. They drove us to a compound outside of Phoenix. There we were unloaded, they gave us access to showers, beds and food. We stayed there for a week. Each day we were interviewed by the patron. He took pictures of us. They gave us dressier clothes for the girls and women and styled our hair. We were also given new names, mine was Desiree. We were relieved to be safe, warm and clean.

First, we were photographed like we used to do in school, sitting on a chair, and happy. We didn't know what the next pictures involved. After they photographed everyone we returned to our bunks. We were happy because we thought they were going to get us an ID card and we would be able to get jobs. The next day the horror started. The pictures were degrading and awful. They asked us to comb our hair and put on makeup. Then we were marched back to have our photographs taken, but this time without our clothes. We were all crying and refusing to get undressed. If we refused they threatened to rape us. Soon almost everyone complied. We were photographed naked and told to smile. How can you smile when you know men are going to see these pictures, people you don't know or even worse people you'll meet. I'm not sure what happened to the women who refused, they didn't return to the bunks that afternoon. We never knew what happened to them.

"Oh, Yasmene. How terrible."

"It got worse. The pictures were sent to sex traffickers up and down the I-5 corridor. They bid on groups of us. When they got a bid for five or six of us they put us in a van and sent us further north. We never saw the others once we left. We were all sent to different places."

At this point, I realize how lucky I was to arrive at Fish Camp without passing through one of these compounds. What if the kidnappers in Caléxico had been successful? Would I have ended up with the sex traffickers? Patty more or less said I barely escaped kidnapping more than once. Yasmene is shaking, tears run down her cheeks and I try to console her. I reach over and pull her in to a hug. There is no way I can imagine the horror she has been through.

"Well, I was sent to Oregon. First to Portland, then over to Vancouver, Washington. I was held captive for three months. Details are too horrific to share, but what I can tell you is I was treated as a sex slave. Because I was younger and not addicted to drugs I was more desirable. I earned a few breaks because they wanted me to stay away from the drugs. That's unusual because drugs were how they controlled us. I also was one of the guard's favorites. On one of those so-called breaks I was able to escape. I spent the first few nights on the streets, my seventeenth birthday I spent on Burnside with other homeless people. It was my saddest birthday ever. Later that week I found a shelter in Portland where I was given medical care and food."

"In the shelter they helped me find a group home. I lived in the group home for a few weeks until one of the workers there offered me a place at her house. There is where I signed up for classes at the local library to learn more English, and she also helped me get some counseling. Things were going so well until one of the sex traffickers saw me on the street one day."

"Oh no, what happened?" I ask.

"Let's just say I was taught a lesson. No dreary details, but that's how I got pregnant. When I returned to my sponsor's home that day she told me about Fish Camp. She thought it was best if I got out of town for a while. She helped me get the job. We are still in touch but if I go in to WITSEC I won't be able to keep in contact with her. Neither of us knew I was pregnant when I came to Fish Camp."

Our hug lasted a long time, no more words but lots of tears. Tears for our shared abuse and loss of self. We were still holding each other when Teodoro came back. I whispered in Yasmene's ear that I would keep her secret. Teodoro leaned in and gave us both a hug. His calming touch helped us both to come back to reality.

He told us of his horrific arrival across the border with abusive coyotes, he didn't need to go in to detail, we knew he had also been forced to do things he didn't want to talk about. Miguel had also been there. Perhaps that is why he said Teodoro was a liar, he didn't want him to tell what really happened to them. We all looked at each other knowing we could all tell more stories, but what would be the point? We were all hurting when we were alone, but together we felt better. There is no way we could be separated now.

"Let's go talk to my family. I need to let them know what we want to do. We need to stick together and help each other. Don't you think?"

"I want that, yes," Yasmene whispers.

"You know that's what I want," Teodoro smiles.

"Okay, let's go talk to them and see when the WITSEC people are coming aboard."

Their first answer is a flat-out no. There is no way they could place non-family members in the same town. It's against policy, is the explanation.

"It's never been done before. We can't take the risk of one of you getting upset with the others and outing them to the public. It's too dangerous, it will never work."

"We need to stay together, we're like family. We have been through so much together we need each other for support," I plead.

"No, it can't happen that way."

"What if we were family?" Teodoro asks.

"What do you mean? The agent asks.

"Like husband and wife, cousins or adopted family?"

I look over at Teodoro, he is so smart. Of course if we get married we can stay together. Did he just ask me to marry him? Did I understand him right? My father's mouth falls open in shock. What is he thinking?

"Teodoro, my daughter is only seventeen. She can't get married."

"With your permission I could Papá"

My mother drops her face into her hands and I hear a sob. Why do they think this is such a bad idea? I am so much more mature now than when I left San Felipe.

"Oh, Sara. Please no. You are so young."

"And how old were you Mamá when you married Papá?"

"Things are different now, hija."

"Are they so different? You were seventeen when you got married. Teodoro, did you just propose to me?"

"Yes, but not officially. I mean, yes."

"My answer is yes."

"Wait a minute, we don't even know if that will work for you to stay together."

"Why not, we will be family. Yasmene and Miguel are my cousins."

"Wait, Yasmene I know you've had some problems in the past and I know you are pregnant but would you like to get married too?" Miguel asks.

"Miguel, you don't know my story. You don't want to marry me."

"Maybe I do. I've had some sad stories too. Nothing I will share here, but I'd be happy to share my life with you. We can share our stories together."

"Okay, wait a minute. Who is the cousin here?" The agent asks.

"I am, Teodoro is my cousin. We came across the border together." Miguel says.

"This all seems a little too convenient. We weren't told this before we came aboard. It sounds very contrived. We'll see what we can do. Give us 24 hours and we'll get back to you," the agent said with a sigh.

As the agents walked away my parents rushed in to give me a hug. "Hija, you don't have to do this. You are so young to get married."

"Mamá, I'm not the same daughter you left behind in San Felipe. So many things have happened and I've grown up a lot. I came across the border with people I didn't know, I traveled by Greyhound to Woodburn, and most of all, I escaped being kidnapped. Teodoro helped me and I have feelings for him.."

"Señores, I understand your concern. I knew when I first saw Sara in the van that we would become friends. What I didn't know is we would someday love each other. If Sara doesn't love me yet that's ok. We'll grow to love each other. I will take care of her, you don't have to worry."

Mary, the WITSEC agent, returns with a briefcase full of paperwork.

"Let's sit down and talk, we have to make sure everyone is clear on what the expectations are. There are so many things to consider."

"We're ready to listen," I answer.

"Okay, there is a possibility of all of you going to the same town."

Cheers erupt in the group and we all hug. My parents look both happy and sad at the same time.

"First, I need to hear from each and every one of you that you agree to participate under your own will. No one is coercing you, no one is demanding you do this. We will interview each one of you individually, including the children. Does that sound reasonable?"

We all agree. My parents look at my brother and sister and tell them they will explain everything later. They seem content to do whatever my parents ask.

"This is how it works. Sara and Yasmene will be involved in some court trials as well as Teodoro and Miguel. The trials will last a few months. Your depositions will be taken via videotape in a courthouse near where you live. Until that is complete we will monitoring your safety and keeping you in a safe house. The process is quite lengthy and for some people it is too difficult and they ask to be released from their contract. You always have the choice to leave, but in this case if one of you leaves it invalidates all of your contracts. We stop protection and all payments, you go back to your old lives. Once you choose to do that you are on your own."

"Sara, your case is different than Yasmene's. Although related, we are prosecuting different people for each case. We may find some of the same people overlap, the cartel uses a lot of the same people along the corridor. The length of each trial could be different. Once one of the cases goes to trial we can start placing you or giving you your options. I can tell you the months running up to your placement are hard, especially with such a large group of participants."

"What if the case goes quickly? Will we be placed sooner? What are the possibilities of my Tío Enrique finding out where we live?" I ask.

"We have an 89% success rate with our placements. When a placement goes wrong it is usually because of a choice the client makes. Let me tell you, we have never had a witness or family member get injured or killed under our care. You will be extremely safe while with us."

"Agent Jackson and I will be your contacts throughout the process. No one else. If anyone approaches you they are not part of WITSEC, do you understand? The FBI no longer will be involved, it will only be the two of us. In the event of our injury or death the WITSEC director himself will contact you. We leave you with a phone number that you can use in that possibility. Let's hope for Agent Jackson and my sake we never have that happen."

"Any questions at this point?"

"How do we go to school or go to work? How do we buy groceries and go to doctors?" I ask.

"Great questions, what I am about to tell you is classified information. I need to get an initial agreement before we continue. Can we first get a verbal agreement before we go to interviews?"

"Can we agree and still change our minds after?" Teodoro asks.

"Of course, you are under no obligation at this point to continue. But, before we give you confidential information we need to have a signature from each of you. Does that make sense?"

"Yes, it does."

"Can we have a private moment before we start the interviews?" I ask.

"Yes, we will be next door. Let us know when you are ready to continue," Agent Jackson answers.

Everyone takes a deep breath and moves closer around the table. We all have questions and concerns and feel vulnerable. Questions come up for us like, "What if I'm the only one who doesn't want to go? What if I'm too afraid? Am I the only one who is afraid?"

My father begins the conversation by saying, "We are happy to be all together again and know what danger you were in Sara. We will do most anything to erase the time you spent alone. If you and Teodoro want to start a new life together your mother and I give you our blessing. We want everyone to stay together. We understand that you also want Yasmene and Miguel to join you. Miguel and Yasmene, we welcome you to our family if you choose to join us."

"Thanks, that means a lot to us," Miguel says.

"Yasmene, how about it. Do you want to join their family with me? Will you think about becoming my wife?"

"Miguel, you are so sweet. I know I need to join this great family. Can we marry as friends first? I may need some time to work through a few things. I don't have any family left except this one."

"Of course, take all of the time you want, we'll work through it together."

"Okay, does that mean everyone is on board to start the interviews? Give a hands up if you are in," I ask.

I look around the circle of my new extended family and see each one raise their hand. My brother and sister also have their hands in the air. It looks unanimous.

"I think we have a yes from everyone. Shall we start the interviews? Or do we have more questions?" Teodoro asks.

"I think we all have questions and doubts, can we agree to meet together when we want to voice problems? If we stay united things will be much easier."

"Group hug!" My little sister Diana shouts.

We all stand and move into a huge hug as a new family. We don't know our new names, we don't know our new placement, and we don't know what the future brings but we know we will be doing it together.

CHAPTER 26

The interviews last until after dinner. We take turns going to the office next to the cafeteria to ask any questions and to be interviewed. The thirty-minute interviews are personal and thorough. We are asked questions about how often we have betrayed a friend, or lied to get something we wanted. These are tricky questions of course because all of us had told a lie at some point in our lives, betrayal of a friend is more difficult. I had to think about what Teodoro might say, or Yasmene. They both had lied to me, that was a betrayal, the agents assured me they were looking for more serious experiences.

Their betrayal in the last six weeks was in a sense to protect me or themselves. Questions also were asked about family and if our family is important to us. So important to fake your death? So important you made your own daughter grieve while you were still alive. I tried very hard to not let the anger boil up iside of me. It had been a horrific experience but I don't know if I would have survived what Yasmene went through. At least now I have my family back, Yasmene will never get back her feeling of safety and trust. She and Miguel will need to work hard to earn each other's trust again. Who knows what Teodoro and Miguel went through before I met them. Today, I don't want to hear any more horror stories. I want to look forward to the future with my family by my side and Teodoro as part of my life.

When the interviews finish Agent Jackson returns to the cafeteria to grab a cup of coffee. We all turn to him with questioning looks and wait for a verdict or answer to our placement.

He holds his hand in the air while pouring his coffee signaling us to wait before asking him any questions. The process of adding cream and sugar to his coffee, stirring the coffee and taking the first sip seems to last an eternity. No sounds except the spoon against the coffee cup are heard. We all hold our breath and wait.

"Get some rest, eat dinner, take a walk. We won't have our decision made until the morning. There are a lot of factors involved and we don't want to make any mistakes. I will let you know you all did very well in your interviews, we just have a few details we need to look at before we can proceed," Agent Jackson says between slurps of coffee.

They hadn't taken time for lunch or dinner during the interviews, they need to eat and rest. I realize the agents are working very hard trying to make this happen.

"Okay, we need to let them work. Why don't we all get some sleep? Nothing is going to change for us sitting here. We all need some down time as well. Today is an exciting day for all of us. We need to find our sleeping arrangements and settle in," I say.

Sleepy eyes and exhaustion meet my suggestion with approval. A crew member came in and told us where to find our rooms. The men were in one room and women and children in another. No one complained or questioned the set up. We all wished each other a good night and settled in for the evening.

My mother and sister shared one bunk while I snuggled with my younger brother in another. We needed to be close to each other, I wish there had been a bed big enough for my whole family, I never wanted to be separated from them again. My brother drifted off to sleep right away and barely moved all night. I tossed and turned trying to calm my thoughts.

First, it all seemed so surreal. One minute I was in San Felipe with my family on the beach, the next they were gone and I was on my own. The trip north, the brief stay in Woodburn with Tío Enrique's family and the last few weeks at Fish Camp. Who could have imagined everything that happened in the last few months? Exhaustion led me to fitful sleep, but I slept for a few hours. Each time I woke I checked to see if my mother and sister were still in the bed next to us and I was still snuggled with my brother and went back to sleep.

We all woke early and rushed to the cafeteria for breakfast. We had eaten very little the day before. Sounds of munching, crunching and slurping could be heard all around the table. We all crowded in to two big tables. Overnight we had become one big family and none of us wanted to be separated again. This was our family and our hope for a future where we could leave our trauma and tragedy behind.

Agent Jackson and Agent O'Malley arrive, exhaustion obvious in their eyes and disheveled looks. A quick hello as they pass by our table without stopping to talk. They were on a mission to get food and coffee and it was obvious they aren't open for anything more than a good morning. They sat at a table away from us and turned their backs so as not to be approached. Their body language was blatant, they might as well have posted a sign with Do Not Disturb on their backs. Sounds of forks and knives filled the small space we occupied. Our table is like a cloud of silence that surrounds us and keeps us unable to speak. No one dares say anything. We look at each other and then back down at the table, each one of us afraid to break the silence.

The two agents stand up, clear their table and turn toward the door. They stop for two seconds to say, "We need to shower and rest. We will be back in 3 hours and then we'll talk."

They leave the cafeteria with a swift G-Man type move, almost too precise. It is like a move they were taught to get out of uncomfortable situations. What could that mean?

Teodoro is the first to speak, "Do you think that is a good sign or a bad sign? Does anyone have a feeling if they are going to let us stay together?"

"No clue, I think we all are confused and hopeful at the same time. What do we do for three hours?" My father asks.

"There's a game room and lounge downstairs. Miguel and I saw it last night. I think we can use it. Let's go there and relax, unless someone else has a better idea," Teodoro says.

We all want to stay together so we move as a group to the game room. My brother and sister find a gaming system and claim it right away. Teodoro and I sit in two lounge chairs and leaf through magazines. Yasmene and Miguel find a quiet place to talk. My parents relax on a sofa out of listening range to give us privacy. I can hear others whispering and trying to have private conversations. We have become a united group so quickly, we haven't had time to speak in small groups. Teodoro and I sit in silence for a few minutes.

Memories of a few short weeks ago when I met him come back to me, he has always been so kind. From the time he offered to help in the van until now, always a gentleman and always helpful. His friendship has helped fill the hole the grief left in my heart. He has been there since I arrived to Fish Camp. I can't imagine living without him or my family. He is now part of my family for sure. The whispers soon became normal conversation and people begin to laugh and forget about our worries. Someone puts on a movie on the TV and we all move closer to watch Swiss Family Robinson, a scary movie to watch while sitting on a ship. Soon we are all engrossed in the story and laughing together. We don't notice when the two agents walk in. They stand and observe us all crowded around the TV on the big sofas, each one squeezing in closer so others can fit. The children sit on the floor, the adults all on the one long sofa with arms around each other.

"Well, we can see you are a united group," Agent Jackson says.

Our heads snap around in unison to see who had spoken. None of us had heard them come in.

"Apaga, hijo," My father tells my brother. My brother jumps up and stops the movie.

"We can talk here or go back next door to the cafeteria, what is your preference?" Agent O'Malley asks.

"Let's go back to the cafeteria, we can sit around the table and hear better," I say.

Once settled at the table and waiting for the agents to begin, I start to cry. The tears run down my cheeks and I start ugly sobbing right in front of everyone. Next Yasmene's sobs could be heard, then my mom.

We are all sobbing when Agent Jackson says, "Stop it now! You haven't heard what we are going to say yet. Why are you all crying?"

"We can't be separated, we just can't. We are all family and we need to be together. I can't stand the thought of being separated again," I say between sobs.

"Okay, maybe if you listen to what we have to say you will stop crying. But I'm not going to be coerced in to making a decision by your tears. Our decision was already made when we we walked through the door."

Teodoro speaks up, "Maybe it's good news, let's listen."

"Smart man. Sara, listen to your future husband."

We all look at each other, "Does that mean what I think it does?" I ask.

"Let's go over a few details before you jump to conclusions. Are you all ready to listen?"

"Yes," we all answer in unison.

"The interviews went well. We have very few doubts about this group. It is in our opinion you all need to be together. Whether or not you accept your placement makes all the difference."

Smiles, cheers and hugs almost made it impossible to listen anymore. We are all so happy we are in disbelief, the tears start again.

"Okay, I'll give you a few minutes to get out the giggles and tears. I'm getting another cup of coffee," Agent Jackson says.

CHAPTER 27

"Let's get the details ironed out, before we make any decisions. We've made the choice of placing you all together in the same town. It makes it more difficult to find a good placement, and it may take a little longer. We have a couple of ideas we will share with you later."

"Because there are three family units if Teodoro and Sara marry and Miguel and Yasmene marry, we can offer more settlement money. It should work out better for you all."

"Miguel, are you sure?" Yasmene asks.

Before Miguel could answer, Agent Jackson says, "Miguel and Yasmene, if you decide to get married in name only we don't need any more information. Your relationship is up to you. As long as you act like a young, married couple to the public, your private life is your own."

"Yasmene, I am sure. But we can take as long as you want to become a couple," Miguel says.

"Like I was saying, there are three couples or family units here. Each family unit receives $60,000 to get settled. This is given to help you through your first six months. We help you find the town, help you locate a house or apartment and give some ideas about finding work and school. In the interviews we got an idea for one of the families. If that works out we can proceed with the placement of the rest of you nearby."

"What is it?" I blurt out.

"Impatient Sara speaks up. You and Teodoro are the two we were thinking about for the placement. What we haven't decided if it would work for you two or for your parents or a combination of both couples."

"What is it?"

"We have a placement in the San Juan Islands, located outside of Seattle in the Puget Sound. It is far enough away from Oregon but still a good placement for you. There is a small Mexican Restaurant for sale on one of the smaller islands. Friday Harbor may be a bit too popular and one of you could be recognized. It's a long stretch that someone would recognize you on one of the smaller islands. Is that of interest to any of you?"

"Yes, I'm interested!" I blurt out without asking Teodoro. I know I can make it work with Teodoro's help.

"Teodoro, what do you think? Are we interested?" I ask.

"I think we can make it work," he smiles.

"Our thought is if you combine your efforts with your Mom and Dad it might make more sense, but that depends on you. There is the possibility of buying a small farm a few miles away. There are fruit trees, a large garden and a small cabin you could rent out for tourists," Agent O'Malley says.

I can see my father's eyes light up. I know he would love a small ranchito, a place he can grow his garden and be outside all day. Teodoro also perks up when they talk about the farm. My mother looks at me with questioning eyes and I nod yes.

"What if my mom and I run the restaurant and Teodoro and my father run the farm? I can see my dad is interested in the farm and my mom is interested in the restaurant. We could all work together."

"It will be up to you to figure out the logistics. We give you the money, help negotiate the purchase of your businesses and a little training. You decide what you want."

"What about Miguel and I?" Yasmene asks.

"Well, there are two options for you. Of course you don't have to choose either one. You can take the money and find a place to live and a job on your own. Like I said there are two choices we can offer you. The first one is a combination bookstore coffeeshop. It has an apartment upstairs where you could live. It is right downtown and close to the Mexican restaurant. The other choice is a bicycle rental and repair shop, that doesn't have an apartment attached and is a seasonal business. Winters would be slow and you'd have less income. The bookstore coffee shop would be open year round and have a local clientele you could build up. What do you think?"

Everyone watches as Miguel and Yasmene smile at each other. It is as if they both know what the other wanted, "We'd like the coffee shop bookstore with the apartment. That will give us the opportunity to be a part of the community. It's perfect."

"Is everyone okay with the suggestions? Or should we keep looking? The next step is to come up with your back story. We need to have a reason you are all moving to the same small island in the Pacific Northwest. But I think we can come up with a story that works."

"What about schools for Diana and Diego?" My father asks.

"There is a great K-12 school system on the island. There is also an outreach community college you can enroll in if interested. The one issue of island living is you can only get there by ferry or airplane. Ferry is cheaper, but you will need to do some shopping off island. When you do that it's more expensive because of transport. But these are details we can work out later. The question you have to think about is do you want to live on an island in the Pacific Northwest where it rains all winter, or do you prefer a city setting? We usually offer you a few choices, but with the number of family members involved the options are limited. It is a small-town atmosphere, people will be very interested in your previous lives so we have to make the story good. In a larger city people aren't that interested when someone new moves to town."

"Will it be a problem? My mom, Diana and my brother don't speak a lot of English. Won't that be an indicator that we are new to the country?" I ask.

"It could be, but we'll come up with a story to help things make sense. Many immigrants take a while to learn English, many never do. We could say your mother was always at home with the younger children and didn't get to know many people. Your brother and sister were homeschooled. Your father's English is limited but he could be an agriculturalist who studied in the U.S. but wanted to move to a place where you all could own your own businesses. There are a number of scenarios we could come up with, once we do you will all have to stick to the same story. The focus primarily will be on your father and how he earned enough money to buy farmland in the Pacific Northwest."

"We'll move forward with the options to purchase the properties in Orcas Island. If we can't secure all of them are you still interested in purchasing what we can? The possibility to get more property may come up in the time we are waiting for a court date."

"Yes, I think we should try to move forward on whatever is available," my father speaks up.

"I agree," Teodoro says.

"Okay, we'll start working on details. In the meantime, when we arrive in Seattle you will all be taken to a safe house. In the weeks before the trial you'll be under Federal Marshall supervision, that means Agent Jackson and I will be your only contacts besides the guards we place outside your door. They will only know they are guarding you for your safety, nothing else. Don't get friendly with them, you don't want anyone who can identify you."

"What will happen to Tío Enrique?" I ask.

"He will be facing twenty years to life depending on the charges. We know the FBI needs your testimony and the evidence you gave to Patty to get a conviction. The FBI has other evidence and they did arrest him with over $200,000 in his garage. There was also physical evidence of ketamine in the garage. Ketamine is a drug used after the kidnappings to transport their victims. There were traces in the garage and also in the laundry room of the house."

"I could have been in the house when it was raided, I touched the drug packet that fell out of his jeans. What if they had raided when I was there? Would I have gone to prison too?"

"Remember Sara, you were being watched. The FBI knew you weren't involved."

"But my fingerprints were on the van and everything. Tío Enrique could have said I was part of the operation. He could have given my name as one of the group."

"But, he didn't and we were protecting you. Get some rest and we'll talk more tomorrow."

Later that night ideas of what Teodoro and I could do with the Mexican restaurant keeps me awake. I know my mother and I can make the best food, but will we be able to run a business? It's something we don't have experience doing, we both love to cook but running a restaurant is something different. I know my father is dreaming of his own farm where he can raise vegetables and have a few animals. I'm not sure how he will make a living, but he and Teodoro will work together. The rental unit will help. Maybe he can raise the vegetables we serve in the restaurant.

Sleep escapes me and the scene from the bus station in Caléxico keeps replaying in my head. What if they had kidnapped me? What if I never made it this far? I might have never met up with my family again or Teodoro. I would be lost in the sex trafficking world. Poor Yasmene, I can't even imagine what she went through. I hope Miguel can help her forget some of the horrific memories. They are good together, I never noticed while on board the ship but they seem happier together. Maybe Yasmene is relieved to be able to tell her story and not hide any more. I drift off to sleep.

CHAPTER 28
Two years later

The restaurant is quiet most mornings. I arrive early to get some quiet time in the kitchen alone. The kitchen work tires my mom out and she prefers to come in later. We usually have coffee together around ten, then begin preparations for lunch. I notice my mother has had a harder time than the rest of us adjusting to our new location. Even the sea air and countryside setting doesn't help. She says she misses the arid climate of Baja. My dad loves our new location and is enjoying every day working in his garden. He and Teodoro work together every morning before coming to the restaurant to help out for dinner time.

All of our produce comes from the farm during the summer months. The order for the materials to build a greenhouse has been sent in. All we have to do is wait for delivery to come on the ferry. Big deliveries only arrive once every two weeks during the tourist season. Teodoro and my dad hope to get the greenhouse built before the rains start in September. They say the warmer temperatures here on the island will allow them to continue growing produce year round. We all hope that will work. We can serve the best product in the restaurant and also save money on the delivery.

Yasmene and Miguel open their coffee shop early and close around three. They seem to be getting along well and have made lots of friends in the community. Their baby, Victor, is almost two now. We all take turns helping with Victor when they have to work late.

Some evenings they hold author nights and invite local writers to come to the island to hold writing workshops. Miguel writes a column in the local newspaper with book reviews and comments about the literary world. Yasmene is writing a novel. She won't discuss the content, but we are all assured we won't be mentioned. We take this to mean she won't discuss our previous life. Victor is the light of her life and has helped her work through some of her previous trauma.

Diana and Diego have made friends with local kids and enjoy the small school they attend. Each morning they board the bus and ride into town to the elementary school. They love the small school atmosphere and both have excelled in their classes.

Their English is improving every day. My mother is the only one who seems to long for our old life.

The apartment above the restaurant has become home for Teodoro and I. Some people in town are amazed that such a young couple owns the restaurant building. It took us a while to become comfortable with our new story. When WITSEC agents placed us here they had quite a solid story for us. We had six months to get comfortable with our new story.

The story is my mom and dad had been successful restaurant owners in San Diego and sold everything to move their family to the Pacific Northwest. They were tired of the out of control property prices and the gang influence in Southern California. They were able to sell their business and property and move the whole family out of California. With the proceeds from the sale they were able to buy the restaurant, farm and coffee shop bookstore. Miguel and Yasmene came with us and make payments to my parents. Teodoro and I also make payments to them. This helps them pay for the farm. At the local bank my parents are the owners of all three properties, but unofficially we all have our own accounts and are working toward ownership.

We need to remind each other constantly to not discuss finances with curious locals. We seem to be a topic of interest and every day people ask us different questions about Southern California. We think they aren't totally sold on our story, but as they get to know us they ask fewer questions. Our food and friendly atmosphere helps them begin to trust us and each day we are closer to becoming part of the community.

The question about my mother and sibling's English comes up quite often. How is it that they don't speak as much English as the rest of us? Does your mother have a learning disability? A learning disability, can you imagine someone asked me that?

I politely say, "Oh no, she is very intelligent. She worked many hours in the kitchen and didn't interact with the customers in the restaurant. She understands some English, but she is more comfortable speaking in Spanish. Here on the island she hears a lot more English, she will learn a little more every day."

"What about your brother and sister? My daughter, a teacher at the school, told me their English is limited. Why don't they speak English?" A nosey customer asks.

"My parents didn't want them to lose their Spanish skills and sent them to a local Catholic school where only Spanish was taught. They are very bright and already speak a lot of English. How about your children, do they speak Spanish?" I ask with a sweet smile.

"Why would they speak Spanish?" The customer replies.

"Oh, no reason, just pointing out that my brother and sister had an excellent education and now will speak two languages. They will have an advantage. It isn't a disadvantage, it's a positive thing to speak two languages."

Our story seems to be accepted by most, but some still come up with those awkward questions. Agent O'Malley and Agent Jackson contact us about every six weeks. Each time they call a different person in our group to make sure they hear from all of us. It's my turn this time. I expect to hear from one of them any day. They call early mornings so not to bother us at work.

Teodoro is still asleep as I shower and get ready for a busy Friday at the restaurant. As I am about to walk out the door my cell phone beeps with a voice mail. I missed the call. I decide to sit down at the kitchen table before going downstairs to begin work. I dial the number Agent O'Malley left for me to call.

"Glad I caught you before you start work Sara, how is everything?" She asks.

"Great, everyone is doing well. We are very busy in the restaurant now that it's summer. My mom and I work during lunch then all four of us are here for dinner. Our dinner hour is very busy...."

Agent O'Malley interrupts me, "Sara, Sara ... I need to tell you something."

"What? I'm telling you everything is going well here. Yasmene and Miguel have a great group of regulars at the coffee shop and …"

"Sara, I have some bad news. Are you alone? Is Teodoro with you?"

"He's in the shower. Why what happened? You can tell me, he is in the other room."

"Go get him now," Agent O'Malley says firmly.

"You are scaring me. What is it?"

"Go get Teodoro now. I'll wait. Then put me on speaker phone."

Teodoro is surprised when I ask him to come to the phone, but stumbles to the kitchen to listen. We know our family is safe because we are all here on the island.

"Agent O'Malley, we are both here. I have you on speaker phone. "What is so urgent," Teodoro says.

"We just got word today. Your Tío Enrique and some of his associates were pardoned today by the president. They will be released within the week."

"What? Can you say that again? I don't think I understood what you said."

"The President of the United States just pardoned your Tío Enrique and some of his associates this morning. You heard me correctly. Your Tío Enrique will be out of prison this week. We assume he will return to Oregon, probably the Woodburn area because he is familiar with the cartel operation there."

"How can he be released? He was sentenced to twenty years to life. It's been less than two years. That's impossible," I stammer.

"We see this all of the time Sara. They have connections to someone very high up and somehow someone owes him a favor. We still don't know who their connection is, but it is someone very powerful to get a presidential pardon."

"What does that mean? Will he be able to find us? Are we in danger?" I ask.

"We don't know. We will watch him to see what he does. At the moment stay where you are, but we may have to move you to someplace farther away. The possibility of him going to Orcas Island is remote, but not impossible. We don't have any leaks within our department. You know Agent Jackson and I are the only two people who know where you are."

"I don't want to leave here, we love Orcas Island. We've made friends here and we are starting to fit in. My mother still struggles with some depression because of the weather, but the rest of us are very happy. I hope we don't have to leave our new home."

"Talk to the rest of your family, let them know what is happening. Come up with a plan of what you want to do. Stay where you are and risk someone recognizing one of you, or relocating the whole family. I'll be in touch early next week. We'll wait to see what your Tío Enrique does when he gets out. The FBI will put an agent on him as soon as he gets back to Woodburn. In the meantime, stick together and continue as normal."

"Act normal? It'll be hard to act normal when we know that psychopath will be on the streets. We'll wait to hear from you early next week. I'm glad you called, but not happy with the news you gave us."

"We are obligated to let you know. It is never good when we have to give news like this to our people. We know you are all doing well there. Your family proved we can relocate such a large group successfully. If we were able to do it once, we'll be able to move you again if need be." Agent O'Malley says.

"Okay." I say quietly.

"Bye, Agent O'Malley. We'll wait for your call," Teodoro says and clicks off the phone.

We ask everyone to meet us at the restaurant. Yasmene and Miguel don't want to close their coffee shop but when we tell them it's urgent they get a loyal customer to watch the cash register. When we share the news with everyone they are all shocked and scared. Yasmene starts to cry as soon as we mention the pardon.

"How can they let those monsters out of prison?" Yasmene asks.

"We can't change any of that now, what we need to do is decide how it will change our situation. What do we want to do? Stay here and risk someone finding us or take the opportunity to move again to another location?"

"What if every three years we have to move? I'm not sure I can do that," Yasmene says.

My father clears his throat and begins to speak, "Yasmene, if our safety depends on a move every three years that is what we will have to do. I doubt my brother can stay out of trouble for very long. He may land in prison again. But, in the meantime we need to make a decision and we need to all agree on it."

Teodoro says, "I agree, we need to do whatever it takes to keep us all safe. I could never forgive myself if anything happens to any of you. We need to really consider moving. Do the agents help us sell our businesses or do we need to do that? I'll call the agents to ask for more details. Maybe we can make a better decision once we are better informed. I'll do that first thing Monday morning."

"Why wait? You know we can call them anytime," I say.

"Okay, let me call them now. They will think it's unusual we call back so soon. I'll grab my phone," Teodoro says.

We all stare at Teodoro as he calls Agent O'Malley. The first call doesn't go through and he redials, "Let me try again, maybe I misdialed," he says as he punches in the numbers again.

"The call doesn't go through. Who has the number? Sara. do you have the number in your phone?" He asks.

"Yes, let me get it. You can call on my phone." I say as I hand him my phone.

"The same thing happens. No answer, no busy signal, no voicemail. Who has Agent Jackson't number?" He asks.

Miguel hands Teodoro his cell phone, "Here, I just spoke with him the other day. He called to ask about our newsletter. He wanted to make sure no one put our picture on the internet. He told us to never post our pictures online. Of course, we already knew that."

"The same thing. No answer. What is happening? We don't have a connection anymore?"

"My phone is ringing. Hello. Yes, let me give the phone to Teodoro," my dad says as he hands the phone over the table.

"Hello"

"This is the Director of WITSEC. I see you have been trying to contact Agents Jackson and O'Malley. I'm afraid I have some bad news. They are both missing. The last phone call they made was to you. Since then they have disappeared. I need you all to grab your important papers and documents. Stay where you are. We have two new WITSEC agents on their way to you now. You are in danger and we have you ready for evacuation to a safe house. Get ready now."

ABOUT THE AUTHOR

Kate Banco lives in the Pacific Northwest with her husband She enjoys travel, gardening and visits to the Oregon Coast. Kate grew up on a dairy farm in Upstate, New York, and moved to Oregon to complete a degree in Spanish and Education at Oregon State University.

Fish Camp is her debut novel. The sequel to Fish Camp will be available in Fall of 2019.

Made in the USA
San Bernardino, CA
01 December 2018